ANGEL ON FIRE

THE WHITEWING CHRONICLES

BOOK 1

CHRISSY DAWSON

Text copyright © Chrissy Dawson 2022

The moral rights of author and illustrator
have been asserted, this book is copyright.

A catalogue record for this book is available from the
National Library of New Zealand.

ISBN: 978-0-473-65478-8

www.chrissydawson.com

CONTENTS

Angels walk amongst us everyday
Normal people like you and me just wanting to do a good deed
Some are of a higher power
Good or evil that is for us to decipher
Angels walk amongst us everyday
Would you know if one came your way?

ANGELA

"Angela!" my dad yelled from the kitchen, interrupting my thoughts. My journal dropped to the floor. "We have work to do, get down here."

My dad meant well, but these days he was consumed by work. I knew he loved me, but lately, I felt like he only wanted me around for my magic ability to see people as they are.

During the school year, I would help dad out where I could after school, or on vacation breaks. Now that I'd graduated, he wanted me to work full-time in his law practice—or, as he called it, the family business. One of my main jobs was to talk to clients. My abilities, from what I understood so far, had a way of showing the good and the bad in people. It was always different, and usually, it was easy to tell if they were lying or not.

When I was around five years old, I remember being upset with Dad about not telling me the truth about Santa, I couldn't understand why he would lie, he didn't understand how I knew he wasn't telling the truth. As I got older it became more apparent, Dad was thrilled,

I have helped him to win some great cases. I don't want to break his heart, but I can't stay here. It's suffocating in this small town.

I want to see what's out there and find out why I have these abilities and maybe find more people like me. What I wanted to do is join the New York Police Academy, I have even put the application in, but the waiting was killing, me it had been a month already. All my friends had already left for college or internships. There was nothing here for me anymore.

Bing bong! My heart fluttered hopefully for a second as the doorbell went off. *Is Mom back?*

"That's Ms. Montgomery. Be nice. She's a new client, and very rich." Dad yelled up the stairs to me. I rolled my eyes, and felt another small wave of hope vanish *she wouldn't have rung the doorbell anyway she would have walked in silly.* I walked down to dad's home office. It used to be one of my favorite places in the house; Mom had furnished it beautifully. Drapes of blue and gold hung down over great bay windows that let in the light and overlooked the orchard. Dad had been so proud. Now he left the drapes closed, and it was a gloomy place with no natural light.

"Please have a seat, Mr. Favorites Montgomery. Thank you for contacting us," I heard my dad say, laying on the charm so thick it was sickening.

I walked in to greet her but the hairs rose on my arms and the blood rushed to my head thumping in my ears I barely heard my dad say, "This is my daughter Angela, she will be helping me with your case." Mrs. Montgomery looked to be in her mid-fifties. Her face was caked in makeup, with bright purple eyeshadow. She smiled at me and relaxed through my assessment. I could barely keep a straight face as I nodded at the introduction. We locked eyes, and pools of black looked back at me. I covered my mouth in horror—her neck was alive! I looked closer, and where my dad would see a patterned scarf, I saw a snake slithering tight against her skin.

My dad looked at me and saw the dread on my face, and I saw a brief look of disappointment before he turned back to her.

"Well," Mrs. Montgomery hissed and to my ears, it was like a snake speaking. "You have a reputation for being the best in this town, and… the most handsome." She smiled at my dad, laying it on as thick as he did, and I almost threw up in my mouth.

"Thank you, we endeavor to represent our clients to the best of our abilities, Angela is a huge help with my investigation work and will make a great lawyer one day soon," My dad said smiling at me and nodding wanting me to say something.

"Yes, my dad is the best there is but I think we're already stretched right now with our current workload, I'm sorry please excuse me". I left the room. I couldn't stand it anymore.

My blood thumped hard in my veins and I could taste it in my mouth, it was different this time, normally with someone evil I get the rush of blood but it is confirmed with a visual picture. It is like I see through any walls or fake images people have built around themselves, to their soul, I can see a person's true self. Mrs. Montgomery is more snake than human but there was something else, she seemed to be a magnet. I wanted to be close to her, to her voice, it was pulling me in. I was disgusted; why would I want to be close to that? I raced back up the stairs and grabbed my journal to write down this strange encounter, and dropped it instantly. "Ouch!" The birthmark on my left palm, which has never given me trouble before, was bright red. I was still staring at it when dad stormed into my room and shut the door.

"What has gotten into you?" he asked in a loud whisper.

"Dad," I said, "we can't help her, she is pure evil." I didn't mention that my birthmark had gone crazy.

"Angel," my dad said. He hadn't called me that in months, not since… I couldn't think about that right now.

"Don't you think maybe you're overreacting a little bit, sweetheart? We need this." His eyes looked into mine, pleading. I couldn't bear to disappoint him.

"Maybe you're right, Dad. Maybe she isn't all bad. What's the case?" I asked.

"She says her son has been accused of murder but is innocent. He's currently in prison, and it will be the death penalty if we don't do anything to help."

"Let me guess, you want me to go to the prison, talk to him, and 'see' if he did it or not? What if he did do it, Dad? Are you still going to defend him?"

"We need the money, Angel."

"There are other cases!" I shouted.

"Yes," he said, keeping calm, "but not with this kind of pay. We will lose the house if we don't do something soon."

The house was a Manor, and we lived just on the outside of a small nowhere town called Red Bridge, mum and dad had this dream for dads practice and an Orchardy. So, when they found this place ten years ago it was an absolute wreck, they lovingly restored it which cost a small fortune.

I sighed, reality hitting. "Ok dad, I know it is been hard, but I don't want to be part of this case, I will just go this once to the prison. It doesn't feel right."

"Thank you," he looked relieved. "Visiting times open in an hour, you can't go in by yourself but the Prison Warden will be there with you. The sooner you start, the sooner it will be over. I will let Mrs. Montgomery know." He walked out of the room, leaving me with my thoughts.

My eyes welled up. *If Mom were here, everything would be okay.* I swiped away at the tears angrily and grabbed my coat. The prison was a mile out of town, so it would take some time to get there.

PRISON ENCOUNTER

I arrived at the prison entrance, slightly nervous. I walked in and let the guards know I was there on behalf of my father. The Prison Warden came out since I was not supposed to see any inmates on death row by myself.

'You again Whitewing' The Warden came out unimpressed. He towered over me, with his grey beard, dark brown eyes on tanned skin, he wasn't exactly mean but he wasn't nice either. 'You're lucky I owe your father a few favors'

We walked down to the surveillance room, inside were a small table and two steel chairs.

'This better not take forever Whitewing, I'm a busy man, The Warden said.

'I got this Warden, I don't need a babysitter, I've done this before I looked up at him in the eyes.

'All right, I will leave some guards outside, don't screw this up' he said and his big boots clomped off.

I sat down on the cold steel chair, I felt him before I saw him. The blood in my veins rushed, and my skin got all prickly. My cheeks flushed. Mrs. Montgomery's son was led in by another large guard, still cuffed, and was placed down at the metal table in front of me. My cheeks got even hotter; he was gorgeous! He was wearing prison orange, and looked about six feet tall, with dark, perfect hair that I was itching to run my fingers through. I quickly regained my composure and shut my mouth, which had been hanging open like a hungry baby bird.

"Guard, you can leave us alone," I said. "I'm sure Mr. Montgomery won't be difficult."

The guard grunted and stood by the door outside.

"Cayden," he said.

"What?" I said.

"My name is Cayden."

"Haha." *Did I giggle? Oh, wow, I want to die right now!*

"Is something funny?" he asked, looking at me with his head on a slight angle and his mouth holding back a smile… that delicious mouth. I shook my head. *Get a grip, Angela, he is on death row.*

"No, no, nothing at all, Cayden." I held out my hand. "Nice to meet you. My name is Angela, and I am here on behalf of White Wing Associates. We are representing you on your case."

He cleared his throat and nodded at his hands, which were still in cuffs. "Oh, right," I said and dropped my hand.

"Angela," he said. *Ahh, his voice is so beautiful when he says my name. What's wrong with me? I have to pull it together.*

"Does anyone call you Angel, for short?" he asked.

I froze, my head finally joining the party. My body, which was totally on its track, was still pumping blood like crazy. He smiled at me, and my body's reaction was just embarrassing. I glared at him, and with an icy tone, I said, "No, I don't like nicknames. Angela is fine."

I opened up the file in front of me, it had a summary inside. Without looking up I said 'Rebecca May, 23 years old was found deceased one week ago with severe burns covering her entire body, so far you were the last to see her and were placed at the scene of the crime.

I looked up 'Did you do it, did you murder her?'

'Do you think I did it?' I looked into his completely black eyes. It was instantaneous like a force field had broken. *Why didn't I see this before?* His skin was alive. Flames jumped up and down his bare forearms where his orange jumpsuit was rolled up. It was mesmerizing. They looked like they were… dancing toward me?

I gasped and pushed away from the table with my hand wincing. I turned my hand over, and on the inside of my wrist my birthmark about the size of a 50-cent piece was red and raised, I had no idea why it was sore. I stood up, and despite my body's protest, went for the door.

"You see them, don't you?" Cayden whispered. I barely heard him through the blood pounding in my ears.

I whipped around my back to the cold steel door. "What are you talking about?" I said.

"The flames. You see them, don't you?" He looked up at me with his black eyes. I should leave, run, get as far away from here as I could, but maybe he has some answers about me. Perhaps he can tell me why I can see the truth behind people's masks, and why my birthmark is suddenly crazy. I need to take that risk.

"Yes," I said, satisfied there was no fear in my voice. "The flames look like they're dancing."

Cayden looked mystified. "Yes, they do that when I'm nervous. Please sit down. I won't hurt you."

"Nervous? You?" I sat back down at the table. "Why would you be nervous? You're the one with flaming skin."

"Yes, let's just call it an occupational hazard that runs in the family. They don't normally dance for people, though. You must be special."

"What do you mean, 'special'?"

"Well, you do have powers, don't you?"

"Maybe" I shrugged.

Cayden laughed "You did just see flames on my skin"

I sighed "I have a unique ability to see people as they are."

"How does it work? How do you see me?"

"It is hard to explain," I said

"Try me"

"Most of the time, it's as fast and easy as a thought to see what a person is; it's visual, as well as a feeling. Everyone is usually a mixture of good and bad; some swing more one way than the other. Their vision of their true selves is always fascinating if they are half good and half bad. Their body would be in two parts; half would be glowing in a white light, all beautiful and smiling, while the other side almost looks like a zombie, slightly dead, lost. It is a bit different each time. There was a case last week where a boy, only sixteen years old, was caught and arrested for shoplifting. When I questioned him, I could see he was a good person except for his hand, which was a skeleton. He was hungry, and his family didn't have much to eat. He did admit he stole some lollies, as well.

"I can't believe I told you all of that, I haven't shared that with anyone, not even my dad'. '

'You didn't answer my question, how do you see…me?'.

I looked into his eyes. Cayden changed into a vision of flames, and I felt hot as if I was in them. I wanted to see what was past the flames, I sensed it was a shield for something more. Wanting to go deeper, it felt right, I hadn't tried it before but I raised my palm in front of his chest and the flames started to part.

"Stop!" Cayden shouted.

I fell back against my chair, my head spinning.

"What did I do?" I said, stunned.

"I didn't think you would get that far," Cayden said, slightly shocked.

"What do you mean? "How did you know I could see your flaming skin; do you have the same abilities as I do?"

"So many questions, Angel." He sneered at me. His soft side had disappeared now.

"I said don't call me that."

"Why did your mother call you that? Do you miss her?"

My mouth gapped open in shock "What do you know about my mother?"

"I know she disappeared, there are still signs on some of the lamp posts, and I know she left you on purpose."

My blood began to boil and this time my face flushed out of anger.

"Do you want to know what I saw when I looked at you?" I leaned in towards him. "A sorry excuse for a man hiding in his mothers' shadows, you're a coward". I pushed back the steel chair which scrapped along the ground.

Cayden stood up "This conversation is over, Guard!" The guard opened the door, 'We are done here, take me back to my cell'.

"Good luck on death row, Mr. Montgomery," I said, he didn't even look back. The guard let me out, and I wanted to run. Instead, I sprint-walked, tears threatening to fall. When I reached the safety of my car, they cascaded down. My mother's disappearance was still too recent and painful to think about;

I was still upset when I arrived at the entrance to our long driveway to check the mailbox. Our signpost read *Whitewing Manor* and hung proudly, swaying in the slight breeze, with two smaller signs under it; *Law Practice and*

Orchardry. Mom loved fruit trees, so the small orchard had oranges, apples, plums, and pears. She would pickle them, stew, bake, and make treats for all the fairs. The fruit now lay all over the ground, rotting. We both hadn't had the heart to pick them this season.

I grabbed a package from the mailbox addressed to me, and drove down the rest of the driveway, relieved to see Dad's car was gone. I couldn't face seeing him right now. I ran up to my room, excited, ripping it open.

Dear Ms. Whitewing, you have been formally accepted into the Police Academy of New York City. Please see enclosed your enrollment pack, and all the information you need.

I read further down. I had to be there in two weeks! *How was I going to tell my dad?* "I got it!" I screamed and twirled around. "I'm going to be a policewoman!"

EVIL

I didn't see Dad last night. He came home late, and I stayed in my room, digesting my enrollment pack—and internet searching what the uniforms looked like, of course.

I was up early, excited. Just thirteen days to go! I had a better bump up my running; the fitness requirement sounded hard, and I wanted to not only graduate but reach the top of my class. I liked to run, anyway. It was a great way to clear my head.

I turned out of our drive to the open road. Next to our orchard was a large vineyard. I loved the look of the vines when they were full of leaves and grapes, all in tidy rows; there was something beautiful about it. Mr. and Mrs. Mackay owned it and were lovely. They often brought samples over to my mom, to see what she thought.

Six months ago, Mom left a note saying that she couldn't do this anymore, that she didn't want this life, and disappeared, at the bottom of the note was an I <3 NY sticker, I never thought much about it at the time. We called the police and searched for weeks and weeks.

There were still some missing posters on poles around the town Cayden had noted. *The police think she committed suicide, but I know my mother. She wouldn't do that to us. I couldn't shake that there was more to it. When I looked into her, she was everything good, her body glowed like golden sunlight, and you just felt happy to be around her. She loved us. I think that's why I refused to grieve, refused to believe she was gone. I think that's part of why I want to join the police. I want to be as close as I possibly can to getting to any information. And even better, I will soon be able to investigate it myself with all the police equipment.* My eyes started to well up again. I had made a loop and was almost back home.

I skipped to a stop. There was a red car I didn't recognize in the driveway; I would've remembered who drove a Porsche in this area. I got closer to the house, and my skin started to prickle, and my pulse quickened I knew who was there. I debated whether to go in. I could keep running and return after she was gone. *Don't be a coward, Angela. You will be a policewoman soon you will face harder situations than this. May as well practice now.*

I walked into our living room removing my ear pods, dad looked very pleased with himself and Mrs. Mongomery was laughing. My body almost jumped for joy to be close to her, but the air was so evil it almost choked me, and Dad was acting like he had a new best friend.

"Oh, Angela. Good, you're back," my dad said, still smiling. "Elizabeth has come with news."

Elizabeth? Since when were we on a first names basis? I smiled at them. Thirteen days to go, just thirteen days to go!

"Nice to see you again, Angela," Elizabeth said in a snake-like voice. "Yes, it's such good news the police have found new evidence that shows that this may have been a suicide attempt and are reviewing that. So, for now,

Cayden is not on death row. It's such a relief."

"I will go down to see the detective soon and get an update on everything. I'll let you know what's new," my dad said.

"That is good news," I said unconvincingly.

"How was your chat with my son yesterday?" Elizabeth asked "he said you stopped by. Thank you for going to see him, he doesn't get many visitors."

"Good," I lied, trying to avoid eye contact with my dad. "I don't think you have anything to worry about." I started to move off toward my room.

"Cayden said you are going to go back to see him this afternoon," Elizabeth continued.

I turned back around. "He did? Oh, I think he was mistaken, I already have this afternoon booked."

"Angel," my dad said, "I'm sure you can move that to another day. This is important, and it would mean so much to Elizabeth and her son."

Thirteen days, thirteen days, thirteen days. I repeated it in my head a few more times before nodding. "Okay, Dad, sure thing. I'm going to go and get changed first." I bolted up the stairs before either of them said another thing.

Back in my room, I flopped onto my bed, and my heart rate slowed down. The prickly feeling subsided, and I closed my eyes. The images of the flames jumping on Cayden's forearms were so vivid. My blood started to pump again. I looked at my palm, my birthmark was still raised. 'I need answers' I said out loud and rolled over out of bed, making my way towards the shower.

ANGELS FOREVER

Cayden sat across from me looking just as gorgeous as before, I was still seething about his comments about my Mother, my body, however, was happily humming a beat with him close by.

"You wanted to see me," I said as icily as I could.

"Yes, I wanted to apologize for how I behaved before; I was out of line."

I didn't expect that and relaxed a little.

"Apology accepted, I'm also sorry, I didn't mean to call you a coward."

"Do you think… I did it? After all, that's why your father sent you here, right?"

"It doesn't matter, we are representing you and will defend you no matter what."

"It matters to me." He put a hand on mine. Because he is no longer on death row, he was uncuffed, and I hadn't even noticed his hands were free.

Despite myself, I looked into his eyes and him. The flames were there but not as hot. I closed my eyes and let my mind guide me, a wall of flames stood strong, I stopped I didn't want to force through but then the flames parted. I heard Cayden suck in a breath. Through the fire, there was a faint golden glow, a softness to him. He was partially good... somewhere.

I sighed and opened my eyes. "No, I don't think you did this, Cayden." I pulled my hand away "My dad will do everything he can, he is very good." I stood up again. "I have to go. We will know more soon. With the new evidence, I'm sure a court date will be sooner, rather than later."

"Thank you," he whispered. I barely heard it. I looked back at him. He had his head down and looked quite sad. I didn't know what to say, so I left.

I should have stayed. I had so many questions, like, how did he know my nickname? His mom could have told him, after all—she had heard my dad say it. But what had he meant by me being special? Or... was he flirting?

I didn't have time to think about it all. I needed to go tell Dad I got into the Police Academy, and get ready to go. Even though I wasn't due at the Academy for thirteen days, I wanted to get to New York a few days before that and do some sightseeing.

I went to Dad's office, but he wasn't there. I decided to wait for a bit and sat in his chair. I used to love playing in here when I was little. The chair was one of those tall-backed chairs, almost like a throne. It had fine blue embroidery on the sides. It looked ancient, and it probably was. When Dad was in court, Mom used to make the chair and the table into a fort, and we used to pretend we were defending a royal castle. Out of habit, my fingers touched under the desk to feel the engraving that Mom and I carved in it: A <3 A, she had said. *Angels forever.* I never once thought about what that might have meant. I just thought it was just Mom's love for me.

The file on the desk caught my eye. It was Cayden's whole case. It had the usual write-up. Cayden was twenty-one years old, six foot one, black-haired, and brown-eyed. It didn't say anything about flames bouncing on his skin, of course.

I turned the page and gagged. A corpse looked back at me. It was a woman with very severe burns. She was almost unrecognizable.

I turned the page quickly. Rebecca May, twenty-five years old. The cause of death is unknown. *How can that be?*

"Angela." My dad walked in. "Are you okay? You're very pale."

"Yeah, I was just reading the complete file and saw Rebecca. Pretty horrible."

"Sure is," my Dad said, "I thought you didn't want anything to do with this? Did you go and see Cayden today?"

"Yes, I went."

"And?"

"I don't think he did it, but I do think he had some part in it."

"Well, you could be right, but we may never know. I just got in from seeing Sam." Sam was our local detective, a nice guy who was never one to give up. "he says that they are considering suicide. She had been having all sorts of troubles at home, and her friends and family described her as a bit lost."

"How could it be suicide if she was burned? what was the cause of death?"

"That's the strange part—we are still trying to figure out the missing pieces. Rebecca was at a rooftop party, but only a handful of people saw her. They described her as agitated and had been crying. Unfortunately, her last known whereabouts had been sitting on a ledge of the roof with Cayden. Were you waiting for me?"

"Huh?" I said. All I could think about was Cayden and Rebecca making out, Cayden's soft lips on hers, his hands holding her in a tight embrace, and then... Rebecca catches on fire. *Whoa—what is wrong with me? Is that jealousy?*

"You're in my chair; did you want something?"

"Oh," I said, snapping out of it. "I had something to tell you." I took a deep breath and looked him in the eyes.

"Dad, I have been accepted into the Police Academy... in New York." I immediately felt a weight lifted off my shoulders. I sunk into his chair.

My dad sat down on the chair in front of his desk. "Well, I'm not surprised."

"What? You're not?"

"Of course. Since you were a little girl, you always had to have the answers to everything, down to the finest detail!"

"I laughed, you're right, mom always said I ask a lot of questions" I looked to dad who suddenly looked so sad.

"Sorry I know we don't talk about her much".

"We should talk about her more" he tried with a small smile. "I miss her too; she would be so proud of you and the Police Women you will become". Tears welled in his eyes.

"Make sure you don't forget to call your old man from time to time."

"Oh, dad!" I ran up to hug him, tears streaming down my cheeks. "Of course, I will be home all the time to visit. I'll make you proud, you'll see. And I bet I can find out what happened to Mom." I felt Dad tense up.

"Just do your best sweetheart, and you'll be fine. I better get back to work. He let me go and moved towards his chair.

"When do you go?"

"Thirteen days, but I would like to go a couple of days earlier to see the city," I said.

"Okay, well I better start looking for another assistant, not that anyone would be able to see people as you do".

"I can still help I promise". I said feeling a bit guilty now.

He looked at me, "I know, but it is your time now, it's time to concentrate on you, do this for yourself ok". Dad said, sitting down at the desk to write up some notes. Dismissed, I left the office.

I should feel happy, and excited, but I didn't. I felt awful for leaving dad and was confused about my abilities, hopefully, New York will also give me more answers about me too.

NEW YORK

I stood in my mirror. The same blue eyes looked back, but I felt different, stronger. I smoothed down an unseen wrinkle from my crisply ironed uniform, and proudly adjusted my shiny Team Leaders badge on my chest.

I pulled out my bun clip and smiled as my long hair tumbled down. *Three months! I made it halfway!*

"Let's go, Whitewing. I need to get out of this place!" Jayla smiled. Her perfect white teeth contrasted with her dark skin and bright red lipstick.

"Got enough makeup on?" I teased.

"Well, I don't know about you, but I need to 'make up' pun intended for lost time and who knows when we will be allowed a full night's leave again?"

I laughed 'Ok only if you promise not to make any more bad jokes like that again' I untangled the strawberry blond strands and plaited through the darker red streak that had always been there since birth.

I hoped James was going to be there. Okay, so he was my Tactics instructor. And I know that meant hands-off. No way was I going to do anything to jeopardize the Academy. But once we graduated… I was sure we had a connection, even though we had barely been alone for more than a few minutes, and that was only in class. The memory of the sensation of him on top of me made me flush even now. Sure, he'd been showing our group how to get out of a defense hold against someone stronger, but the feeling of him lingered. While at the Academy I have decided to strengthen my investigation and research skills as well as learn combat and all of the other parts of training without using my magic abilities. With dad, he and I both relied on them too much and I got tired of being an instrument. Sometimes I regret it, I would love to 'see' into James.

I grabbed my blue top for tonight from my bed. A letter dropped from underneath it. I picked it up. It was from Dad. I still felt homesick, so I looked forward to Dad's letters each week. He said he was ok, still looking for an assistant to help him which made my stomach churn in guilt. Cayden was still in prison but the trial will be soon. Dad said the verdict was looking good.

"I bet Mike will be there," Jayla said, twirling her hair. "He's so hot!"

Pulled from the letter, I laughed again and turned to Jayla. I loved that about her; she always made me laugh.

Jayla Price, my roommate, had become my best friend even though she was my polar opposite. She came from a wealthy family, was the youngest of four children, and was rebellious. Her parents had big expectations of her to 'make' something of herself, just like her older two brothers and sister, and they were horrified she joined the Academy. At first, that was why she did it, but I knew she loved it here. She constantly flirted with every instructor and cadet and even received a warning for her behavior. She was incredibly beautiful and knew it. She had passed everything so far with minimal effort. I could tell she was smart but only wanted to put in the smallest amount of work necessary.

Jayla smoothed down one of her long black curls. "Let's do this!"

We turned up to a club that was popular with Academy cadets. We had to avoid public socializing while in training, in case any incidents occurred. I immediately scanned the room for James.

"He won't be here, Angie," Jayla said. "Instructors don't socialize with cadets. It's against the stupid rule book; they can't have any fun."

"Huh?" I said, defensive. "I knew that I was just looking to see who was here."

"Well, this isn't a funeral. Come on, let's get drinks!" Jayla shrieked as she bounced over to the bar.

"Shots, bartender, and keep 'em coming!" Jayla said as she grabbed my hand, and I couldn't help but be caught up in her infectious energy.

"Hey, Jayla Bug, can I buy you a drink?" Reggie, the class creep, sneered, fawning over Jayla.

"Beat it, Reggie, and don't call me that."

"Here, Angie," Jayla passed me a shot glass with oozy green liquid.

"Why did you bring this teacher's pet loser with you?" Reggie smirked at me.

I felt my blood begin to boil and opened my mouth to defend myself.

"Ignore him," Jayla said. "Come on, let's get a booth over here and get some more drinks." She pulled me away from the bar.

Fuming, I asked, "What's his deal, anyway?"

"Oh, he is just pissed off, Angie. You took his precious Team Leaders badge and a free ride through the Academy from him, when he thought it would be rightfully his."

"We can't even report him, which is so frustrating. I hate putting up with his crap," I said.

"Yeah well, we don't want daddy Police Commissioner's nose bent out of shape, and we don't want to be put on the radar when we haven't even really started yet. Just forget him. Here, has another shot." Jayla shoved another shot glass at me, this time of bright blue liquid. I gulped it down, determined not to let Reggie ruin my night.

"Hey, gorgeous ladies!" Mike and Pete slid in next to us in the booth.

"Oh, hey Mike," Jayla purred, fluttering her eyelash extensions.

"Hey, Whitewing," Pete said, smiling at me. "Good to see you out."

I smiled back. Pete was cute enough, but he was no James.

"I don't think I had a choice" I laughed looking in Jayla's direction.

"Ouch?" Jayla had just kicked me hard under the table, pleading eyes staring into mine. I rolled my eyes. *Okay, fine, I'll play along for you.* I stared back just as intently.

"Yeah, it's great to be out! Let's get some more drinks!" I said, a bit too loudly.

The jukebox started up, and I let myself soak up the surroundings. I smiled at Pete, who had just made a terrible joke, and at Jayla, who sat there looking at Mike adoringly as he put his arm around her. I felt happy, truly happy, for the first time since I couldn't even remember when. I had friends and felt like I fit in. This week we had finally been shown the Police database and where to find out criminal information, my mind was swimming with questions and I wanted to get time to research my mother's case. We weren't allowed to access the system by ourselves yet but the campus librarian seemed happy to show me. I felt like there was some hope in finding her. I couldn't mention it to dad yet, I will wait until I have something to show.

I downed another shot of liquid Jayla shoved my way—this time red—and licked my lips that tasted of cherry. I got up to use the girl's room and swayed a little. *Okay, that's my last drink for the night. I need some fresh air.*

Out in the alleyway, I closed my eyes, leaned against the cold brick wall, and felt the music vibrations along my back.

My blood started to thump, and it wasn't from the club.

Cayden walked out of the shadows, gorgeous as ever, smiling, but it didn't reach his eyes. "Angel, I didn't expect to see you here," he said sarcastically.

"Cayden?! What?! How?! I was doing my best to ignore my body, but the blood pumping in my ears was blaring like trumpets as he got closer.

"I just read my dad's letter and it says you're going to trial soon does the prison know you're here? I'm in the Police Academy now, and I have to bring you in if you're a fugitive."

"They brought the trial forward thanks to your dad's insistence and I was released, not enough evidence to keep me".

"Oh, I mean congratulations, what was the conclusion for Rebecca?

Cayden's eyes went black "Suicide".

I nodded "You came all this way to tell me? I need to get back" I turned around and reached for the door.

"Wait, please." He put his hand on my shoulder.

A bolt of electricity hit me. I gasped and turned around in shock.

"Angel, you're in danger. You need to be careful," he said looking concerned.

Getting my voice back I replied, "What are you talking about Cayden, why would I be in danger, and why should I trust you?"

"This is not the place to explain everything, can we meet somewhere"

"I'm in training Cayden, we are not allowed to just wander out when we feel like it, this is our first evening out in three months."

Cayden looked frustrated but concerned.

"Look whatever it is I'm sure I will be fine after all I am in the Police Academy, what safer place could there be?"

"You don't understand," he said pleading.

"This is serious"

There was a loud creak, and the alley door swung open. "Angie, are you out here?" Jayla popped her head out into the alley.

"Oh, there you are. Are you okay? I got worried when you didn't come back."

"Yeah, I'm fine. I was just talking to…" My words trailed off, as Cayden disappeared. "…Ah… oh, nobody. I was just getting some fresh air. Those shots are strong!"

"Well come on, we're going to do some karaoke!"

"No way, you're not going to get me up there."

"Please, Angie, you know how much I want to impress Mike!"

I sighed. "Okay, just for you…just this once." I grabbed the alley door handle.

"Ouch!" My palm was on fire. I looked down, and my birthmark was bright red. Jayla was already bouncing back into the club and—lucky for me—didn't notice.

The flames consumed me; I was part of them, and they were part of me. All power, all energy. But I was alone, frightened, and didn't know how to find my way home. I opened my mouth to scream.

I woke abruptly in a pool of sweat. The morning alarm was ringing to alert the cadets for our dawn run. I was disorientated for a second. Cayden came first to my mind, then the flames. I patted my body to make sure I wasn't on fire and jumped out of bed. My head spun, and my tongue stuck to the roof of my mouth. "That's the last time I let Jayla take me out," I grumbled. "I bet I'm not going to win any best times today."

"Get up Jayla, you're going to be late," I said, shaking her.

"Ow, what truck hit me?" Jayla groaned as she tried to sit up.

"You only have yourself to blame. It was those last orange shots you downed."

"You should have stopped me!" Jayla said.

I laughed. "And would that have worked?"

"Well, no, true. Okay, fine." Jayla flopped back down. "I'll meet you there. Start without me."

"Don't be too long; you already have a warning," I said, putting my shoes on.

I shivered as I stepped out into the morning fall air. The hairs on my arms stuck out. It was so quiet, too quiet. My blood started thumping, my skin got all prickly, it was like I was going to black out, I felt faint and dizzy, and just when I thought I would pass out a flame wall enveloped me. I threw myself on the ground and rolled around like we were trained thinking it was a real fire, terrified, and images of Rebecca came to my mind. I sat up and started to pat down my arms, and saw that the flames were caressing my skin, I wasn't actually on fire. They were traveling up and down… from my birthmark?

"Whitewing! Resting already?" James asked.

"Huh?" I blushed and stood up. The flame wall was gone.

"Let's go, Cadet. I was rounding up the last of the stragglers, looks like you're all struggling this morning." James said, and he started to jog off.

"Yes, Sir," I mumbled, catching up with his stride.

"Did you enjoy your night's leave?" James asked as I got closer.

I was surprised; this was the first time he had asked me a question that wasn't to do with training.

"Sure. Well, until Jayla made me do karaoke," I replied.

James laughed. "I would have liked to have seen that."

"No really, you wouldn't. I sounded like a screeching cat—well, to my ears, anyway."

"I doubt that. I'm sure you would have sung like an angel," James said smiling at me.

My heart did a stupid flutter and I know I had a goofy smile on my face.

"Wait up!" Jayla shouted before I could reply. The sun was now just peeking over the horizon of the training grounds.

"Ms. Price, how nice of you to join us," James said, smile gone.

"Sorry, sir!" Jayla said, puffing.

"You will all receive an extra lap this morning, and I hope you think about how to be responsible next time. Even when you take leave, you still represent New York's finest, and you need to act accordingly." James said as he ran off to gather the rest of them.

Jayla stopped out of breath. "Well, he sure is in a grump this morning, isn't he!"

I stopped too but didn't reply. I wasn't ready to share the chat I just had and more than that, I needed to find out why my skin was flaming.

The weeks flew past as training ramped up my flaming skin hadn't returned but in its place were flaming nightmares instead.

The morning alarm rang. I groaned and sat up.

"You had another nightmare, didn't you?" Jayla asked.

I had to tell Jayla about the nightmares as she was getting concerned and almost told James, she didn't know the full details, just that they were scary and reoccurring.

I pushed back the covers. "I'm fine."

"Angie, please. It's been a few weeks. I know I said I wouldn't say anything, but you look weaker by the day. You should go to the medics they can help."

"I don't want to talk about it. It's probably just homesickness".

"Okay well, it's your funeral," Jayla said with deep concern in her eyes.

Stepping out into the morning air, I took a deep breath enjoying the chill; lately, I felt hot all of the time.

We slowly jogged over to the outdoor running track, the sky was still dark but it was clear and I could tell it would be a gorgeous day. The Police Academy had 32 acres of grounds but was still in the heart of the city, there was also a running track indoors when the weather turned but I loved being outdoors. James was already there doing his warm-up stretches. I couldn't help but notice his muscular shape beneath his thin running top.

"Sweating already, Whitewing? Afraid to lose your best time?" Reggie said.

"Butt out, Reggie," Jayla replied. "At least she has the best time to beat."

"You do look unwell," James said. "Do you want to sit this one out? You can make it up another day."

"I'm fine. Let's go." "Okay, cadets, line up," James commanded. "On your marks, get set, go!"

I felt good and was leading the pack in the first mile. The sun was starting to come up, and the sky was a vivid, burnt orange. What was it that Dad always said? 'Red sky in the morning, shepherd's warning?' My mind drifted to Dad, I hadn't texted him in the last few weeks, and I made a mental note to call him tonight.

An intense pain hit my chest as I rounded a bend on the second mile. I couldn't catch my breath and slowed down but didn't stop running. Other cadets raced past me. "Ouch!" I said as Reggie clipped me on purpose as he ran past me.

"You snooze, you lose, Whitewing," he called back.

Jayla came up. "Are you okay? You need to stop. I'll get help."

"No, don't you dare. I'm fine, just catching my breath. Go on without me."

Jayla looked at me, her eyes pleading with me to stop, but she said nothing and carried on.

More pain hit me, it felt like my ribcage was trying to push out of my body, I fell sharply to my knees.

James rushed up. "Angela! What is it?"

Unable to speak, I clutched at my chest and doubled over in pain.

"I've got you. This is not the way you finish my course," James said as he scooped me up like a feather. I tried to protest, but the pain was too intense, and it all went dark.

I was surrounded by flames, but beyond the ring, I could see darkness, that is what I wanted, peace, to have no pain, no thoughts. I reached for the dark, for it to end. My birthmark started to glow, and I shielded my eyes.

"Angel, I know you're in there. Come back to us."

"Mom?"

I felt myself being pulled towards the fire. "No, I don't want to go back," I said and reached again for the darkness.

"Angel, please we need you, I need you, come back, don't give up yet."

There were so many flashes. I was running through the orchard with Mom. I must have only been about five years old, and we were laughing, and happy. Then, we were at my house.

There was a Christmas tree, and music playing in the background. Mom and Dad sat by the fire, looking at each other with such love. A voice echoed around me.

"I've got you, Angel. Just try, please."

More flashes, now I saw Jayla, Cayden, and James. I couldn't leave them, not yet.

I let myself be pulled into the flames, expecting pain, but there was none. I opened my eyes. Everything was blurry, but slowly gaining focus.

Cayden came into view. He looked ashen, drained.

"There you are," he whispered, "I thought I was going to lose you."

"Cayden? Why are you here?" I looked around and saw Dad in the corner, slumped over a chair snoring.

"Where am I? Why is my dad here?"

"Shhh, it's okay. It's the middle of the night. I snuck in. I knew I had to save you," he said.

"You saved me? From what, Cayden?" I tried to sit up, and my head spun.

"Whoa, slow down, Angel."

"Okay, you have some explaining to do. Get talking, now, and don't call me that!"

He sighed. "Okay, please keep your voice down. You have fire fever, and if you don't let me help you, you'll die."

I saw in his eyes that what he said was the truth, and lay back down… carefully.

He relaxed a little and sat back down next to my bed. I noticed that he was holding my hand and pulled it gently from his grip, absently rubbing my birthmark.

"I'm tired, I want to sleep," I whispered, and started to close my eyes.

"You need to hear this—there won't be another chance, once morning comes," he said." There is no easy way to say it, so I'm just going to come out with it; you're a demon."

I tried to sit back up, but he put his hand on my shoulder firmly and gently.

"Wait, that's not all. While you have been at the Academy, you have chosen to suppress and ignore your demonic powers, despite the signs that I'm sure your body has been giving you."

"The fire," I said, my voice wavering. I started to close my eyes.

"No," he said in an urgent whisper, "you can't sleep yet. If you do, the darkness will take you."

"I don't want the fire, I don't want it," I said, as tears streamed down my face.

He tenderly held my hand again.

"I'm here, Angel. I will help you. I'm also a demon, a good one." He smiled a cheeky grin. I couldn't help but give him a small smile back.

"We will go slowly. I will guide you."

I nodded, feeling fainter by the minute. "Ok Cayden, what do we need to do?"

"We don't have much time. It sounds big, but for now, all you have to do is look inside yourself and embrace your fire. Then you can sleep. I am holding the darkness away for now, but to be honest, I don't think I can do it for much longer. You've got to help me on this one." He smiled again, but it was weaker than the last one.

"Okay," I whispered. "I'll try."

"Keep holding my hand so that if it gets too much, I can try to pull you back. Okay?"

I nodded and closed my eyes.

The fire, like my dreams, was powerful. Instead of running like I always did, I made myself really see it, really look into it. I was in the center of a ring, and it was around me wanting, waiting. My birthmark thumped, and I stroked it. The circle started to hum, but something was wrong—the humming quickly turned into a wail. I reached out to touch the fire; it was in pain and suffering. Beyond the ring, the darkness was closing in and pushing hard against the fire, to get to me.

Angry, I held out my arms to embrace my fire, I understood now, it wasn't my ribcage trying to leave my body it was my fire trying to find a way to escape the darkness. "I'm sorry. Let's protect each other!"

The fire ring spun around faster and faster until it was a coiling blur. There was a gigantic blast of light.

I opened my eyes.

Rays of sunlight streamed through the blinds. Cayden was gone, and my dad was sitting next to me, holding my hand.

"Angel," he said, tears glistening in his eyes.

"Dad?" I asked.

"You had me worried, kiddo," he said. "When they called me to say you collapsed, I came as fast as I could."

"Oh, Dad!" We hugged.

"I'm going to be okay," I said, tears on my cheeks.

A nurse came in. "Welcome back, Angela. I just need to do some check-ups, sir—if you could step back for a bit."

The nurse, —large in stature, but surprisingly gentle in her assessment—was quick and orderly.

"I think you're one lucky girl. You had a severe fever. We thought we were going to lose you. It looks like you'll be fine, but we want to keep you one more night, just to be safe," she said.

"How long was I out for?" I asked.

"Two days, honey," the nurse said.

Two days?" I sat up immediately, reaching for the covers. "I need to get out of here, I'm going to be in so much trouble. I need to get back to my training before I get kicked out."

My dad came back to my side. "Angel, it's okay, please rest. They understand. Your teammates were so worried about you that they have been camping out in the waiting area since you collapsed. "he said.

Tears streamed down my face. "They did that for me?"

"They sure did," James appeared at the door. "It is great to see you're ok". He grinned at me and came up to the bed.

"James…" I started to say.

"You don't have to apologize, Angela, we all get sick."

"No, I… thank you for saving me. The nurse said I was lucky."

He touched my arm. His hand was nice and warm. "You scared me—*us*, Angie." For a moment, his face showed his genuine concern. "Don't do it again, okay?" He laughed.

I smiled back.

"Yes, sir!"

"Angie!" Jayla shrieked and bounced in. "They said we could see you!" She hugged me fiercely.

"Poo, you stink Jayla," I laughed.

"Yeah, well, you would too if you camped out here for a few days. I didn't want to leave in case something…" Her voice trailed off.

"It's okay," I said. "I'll be fine. Just another night, and then I'm out of here."

Mike, Pete, and surprisingly, Reggie came in.

"Damn Whitewing, you will do anything for attention!" Reggie said, smiling.

Everyone laughed.

The nurse came back in. "Okay everyone, that's enough for one day. Out you go, especially you four." She said.

I pinched my nose in mockery at Jayla, Mike, Pete, and Reggie. "Will you *please* go now, and have a shower?"

They all mumbled but didn't disagree. Jayla gave me one last hug, and they all left. My Dad and James were the last to go.

"I will come and check on you in the morning, okay, Cadet?" James asked.

"Angel, I will be back in a few hours," Dad said.

"Okay," I replied, and lay back down.

The quiet was soothing. I felt weak but alive. I looked down at my arms and saw bright flames moving under my skin. I closed my eyes, and the fire was there—my fire. It hummed happily. *I won't ignore you again. Let's figure this out together.*

I rested, longer than I intended to. When I next opened my eyes, it was nighttime again.

My birthmark started to warm and my skin started to prickle. I was still getting used to all of the signs of my fire but I was pretty sure I knew what this one meant.

"Cayden," I said. "Are you there?"

"Hi, Angel," Cayden said as he stepped out of the shadows. "You look a million times better."

"I need some answers."

"I bet you do," he replied. "You're still weak, so I will only answer a few, at this stage. Now that you're safe, and I can see by your skin that you and your fire are friends, you're out of immediate danger, for now,"

"Why didn't you stick around? Why all the sneaking in and out?"

"Well, you are new to this but I don't think trying to convince your dad, the hospital, and The Academy that you're a demon and I was trying to save you would be a great way to introduce myself, do you?"

"Oh well when you put it like that, you could have come during the day though, like a normal person to visit".

"I could have but I was exhausted! It was a team effort you are sitting here bright and chirpy you know" He looked a little hurt.

"You're right, I'm sorry, I never did say thank you," I said and this time I took his hand.

"Thank you for helping me through my fire Cayden, I wouldn't be alive without you."

He seemed satisfied and smiled "Your welcome, what else you got?"

"Your mother… she's also a demon, isn't she?" I asked, quickly.

"Yes, she is," he said.

"And I can see things because I'm a demon?"

"Yes, that's right."

"But so, then you can also see people as I can?"

"All demon powers are slightly different, and some are more powerful than others. So, no my mother and I cannot see people like you we have never met another Demon who can."

I wanted to ask more about demon powers but needed to ask the hardest question.

"My mom was… is… she a demon, also?"

"No, I don't think she is, Angel, but I don't know everything," he said.

I got a sense he wasn't telling me everything.

"I think that's enough for now," he said. "We will start training when you're a bit stronger."

"Training?" I asked.

"Yes. You don't want more fire fever, do you?"

I shuddered. "Hell, no!"

"Well, then I need to show you some tricks of the trade," he said. "Good night, sleep tight, don't let the firebugs bite." He smirked. "I will be in touch."

And with that, he was gone. The last thought I had as I drifted off was about Cayden referring to my mother as if she was still alive. What was he hiding?

TRAINING

The moonlight streamed through the trees, illuminating a path down to the target training area. I told Cayden to meet me down here as there were many acres of land around the buildings of the academy and the trees provided great cover and it was the furthest point from the sleeping quarters.

I could see Cayden with his back to a tree, his eyes closed. I felt him though before I saw him my birthmark heated up and my skin prickled.

"Cayden, I know you're there," I said in a loud whisper in case anyone was around.

He popped out from behind the tree smiling.

Wow, he said assessing me, you look…relaxed.

I flushed which I hoped he wouldn't notice in the shadows of the trees, my hair was out of the usual bun or plait and hung loosely around my shoulders, since the fire fever my red streak across my temple was brighter. Jayla had even asked if I was using a new hair conditioner.

He looked at me like a hungry wolf and grinned.

"I feel relaxed, but more than that I'm alive."

"Ok, well, ready to learn from the best?"

"Yes," I nodded slightly nervous. "How many lessons will we need?"

"I guess it depends on how well you listen and practice, you could be a horrible demon."

I smiled; he was teasing.

"I love a challenge.

He stepped closer to me and traced his finger up and down the inside of my arm, caressing the pattern of the flames. We both felt my blood following his finger like a purring cat.

"Every demon's power is slightly different, they're a gift. and they're part of who you are. And if you don't release the energy… well, you saw what happened, fire fever can be fatal, once you get it you need another demon or two to help pull you out of it."

He pulled back, and we both felt the separation and I saw it in his eyes, I let out my breath not even realizing I was holding it.

"Let's start with the rules about using your powers."

"There are rules?"

"Of course. We can't just go around flaming people, what did you think?"

"Well, to be honest, I hadn't thought about it."

He indicated a seat nearby for us to sit.

The trees rustled overhead as a breeze picked up, and a cloud blocked the moon. Everything fell into darkness.

Cayden picked up my hand and turned it over.

Quietly, he said, "Every demon has a mark, a calling card." He stroked my palm, and my birthmark started to glow, illuminating them.

"I always thought it was just a birthmark," I said amazed. "Where's yours?"

"Mine is also on my palm," he said, as he turned his hand over.

"Do all demons have them on their palms?" I asked.

"No," he said. "I have never heard of another demon with one there, until you."

"How did you make it glow like that, it gets hot and raised for me but I haven't seen it glow".

"I will show you in our training sessions, your mark is where your power is unleashed, like a gateway between worlds".

My head started to spin with questions, the cloud moved away from the moon, and they were covered in the moonlight once more.

I looked down afraid to ask but my heart needed to know.

"My father… he's not a demon, is he?"

"No, he isn't," he said, not sugarcoating it.

"So, who is my father?"

"I can't answer that question Angela" He looked away.

"What, why not?"

"When I said there are rules of using your powers, there are also rules about what you can and can't talk about, this is one of those"

"Ok great so now I don't know where my mother is and I don't know who my Father is," I said feeling pretty sorry for myself.

"But you're alive, and you know who you are". Cayden said.

I thought on that for a few minutes before asking another question I had wanted to ask since meeting Cayden at the Prison.

"Cayden… what happened to Rebecca? I saw the photos of her body. Did you…"

"Murder her?" he said.

"No… I know you didn't do that. But did you accidentally set her on fire?"

Cayden stood up, his back to her. It was a few minutes before he spoke.

"We had gone out a couple of times. My parents had warned me not to date a human and that there would be consequences but I liked being with her. She was smart and witty, and a great way to piss off my parents."

He turned around with a look of genuine remorse on his face.

"But we were fooling around, and she wanted to…" He looked away. "Be intimate together." He had tears in his eyes, now. "I never meant to hurt her! I let go of control, and…"

I stood up. "It's okay. You don't have to say anymore." I grabbed his hand and guided him back to the bench.

We sat in silence for a while before I said, "It wasn't your fault, it was an accident."

"I know, but she was innocent," he said in an almost whisper. He shook his head, and his demeanor shifted.

He stood up again and let go of my hand." I understand if you don't want to train anymore tonight"

I stood up too, "I still do of course, or are you afraid I will beat you on my first try?"

He gave a hint of a smile, "Ok just one simple action and we will call it a night."

"Sounds good."

He turned toward me and held out his palm and a flame popped out of nowhere.

"Wow," I said, how did you do that?

"With practice and concentration to start with then it will be as simple as thinking, this is your fire, you need to master this flame first then once you get the hang of it, you can do much more fun things."

His flame grew into a ball then several balls and he started to juggle them.

I grinned, excited, and held out my palm, doing my best to concentrate a slight sweat broke out on my forehead and finally a tiny flame popped up before disappearing.

"I did it!"

Cayden laughed and shook his head, "I don't think I have seen anyone do it on their first go, well done!"

We stood there smiling at each other for a few seconds.

"Oh well I think that's enough for tonight, you should go rest we don't want to push you too much."

I nodded, "Ok, can we do another session again soon?"

"Yes, I will let you know, bye Angie, great work tonight". He turned and started walking towards the trees.

I watched him go then started to walk up the trail back to the dorms practicing my fireball, on the third attempt my biggest one yet materialized and I got so excited I turned around and ran down the hill hoping Cayden hadn't left yet so I could show him the huge fireball.

I stopped in my tracks as I heard voices, I couldn't see them under the canopy of the trees.

"I haven't heard from you in weeks, and I need to know how plans are progressing with finding her Mother Gavriel."

Whose voice was that I wondered if it sounded so familiar.

"This is just a game to you, isn't it? Angela isn't just another notch in your belt, someone else to be used. She is..."

"What is she Cayden? Don't tell me you're falling for her!"

"She needs to trust me, so I have to be careful and go slow. That takes time."

"We don't have time, son."

Son! It was Mrs. Montgomery; I knew I had heard that voice.

"Get it done… or I will."

It went silent and I couldn't believe what I just heard; this was all an act? I should never have trusted him! Furious, I charged the rest of the way down to the canopy.

"Cayden Wh…" I started to say.

He leaped into the air and shot out a flame, which sped at lightning speed toward me.

Without thinking, I quickly put up my hands, and a shield covered me. His firebolt bounced off and slammed into a nearby tree, making a smoldering black hole.

"How did you…?" he started to say.

"How did I…?" I said at the same time.

We looked at each other and burst out laughing. We laughed so hard tears were in our eyes.

"You should have seen your face," I said, still laughing.

"Mine? You should have seen the shock on yours!" he said. He sat down on the mossy ground.

"Look at what you have done to that poor tree!" he said, pointing at the tree but grinning.

I sat down too. "Me? You're the one that shot a flame at me. Which, by the way, was pretty cool. Can you teach me how to do that?"

"Well, by the looks of things, I think you have it all under control. Maybe you should be teaching me."

I laughed. "I have no idea how I did that!"

They both went silent, still grinning and out of breath.

"Why did you come back?" he asked.

"I heard you…and your mother Cayden." Blood rushed to my face, furious again.

"What did you hear?" He asked concerned.

"Something about you running out of time, and you have to get it done or she will, it was about me wasn't it Cayden? What's going on?

He sighed.

"Your right it was my mother and her horrid pet snake that hates me, probably my fault, I haven't been to see her in a while."

"Does she know I'm a… demon?"

"Yes, she does. We both knew as soon as we met you."

"You did?" I stood up. "Why didn't you say something?"

Cayden stood up too but leaned against the tree. "I wanted to. I tried to when you came to see me in prison those times. I just couldn't find the words, and you seemed like you had a lot going on with your mother, and everything…"

I walked over to the scorched tree, tentatively touching the burnt area.

"I thought you were hiding something when I looked inside you. There was something you were holding back. That would have been a lot for me to deal with." I turned back around to him. "But that wasn't your decision to make. You should have told me".

"I'm sorry," he said. He walked towards me. "I also wasn't in a good place. For the longest time, whenever I closed my eyes, all I could see was Rebecca's poor, charred body. The guilt was horrible. It still is."

I relaxed my shoulders, I did feel sorry for him, especially about Rebecca.

"I really should get back to my dorm, I still have more questions though.

"Yeah, it's getting late. Do you want me to walk you back?"

I laughed. "No, I think I'll be okay."

He laughed, too.

I turned around to leave but looked back at him. "Same time tomorrow?"

"I'll be here."

I walked back up the hill.

I walked back to my dorm, pondering the evening with Cayden, I really wanted to believe him but the more questions I asked the more suspicious I was getting, his story wasn't quite adding up. The moon was still full as I got closer to the buildings. My fire was prickly on my skin and my mark was still tender. "You like him, don't you?" I asked the flames, as I watched them swirl.

"Who do you like?" James asked.

I jumped raising my hands ready to make a shield wall. "Oh, don't do that! You frightened me."

He grinned. "Sorry, didn't mean to scare you".

"What are you doing here? It's the middle of the night."

"I might ask you the same question, cadet. I'm on patrol tonight. I was doing my rounds when I heard you."

James walked closer to me. I could smell a mixture of sweat and cologne on him. His short hair, a mousy brown, looked golden in the moonlight, and his green eyes looked bright with mischief. He was a good head taller than me, so I had to tilt my head back to look at him.

"I couldn't sleep, and thought a walk might clear my head," I said.

"You know cadets aren't supposed to leave their dorm at night."

"What if I wanted to live a little dangerously," I said looking up at him and smiling.

"Well, you might get in a lot of trouble". He replied moving closer so our bodies were almost touching.

"What if I want to get in trouble," I said voice husky.

He reached down and touched my cheek.

Before I could respond, he leaned down and softly kissed my forehead, then my nose. I felt his tongue do a soft lick on my earlobe. I giggled.

"I can stop there if you want me to," he whispered in my ear, then tickled me with his tongue. I cupped his face in my hands and brought his mouth to mine. He kissed me gently at first, but I wanted more. I grabbed his shirt and pulled him closer.

He responded by pushing me back against the nearby wall. I made a little groan, and he hitched me up, so my legs were around his waist. I groaned more as our tongues met.

My internal fire matched his passion, and my blood started to pump. He moved his hand down my body, and our kissing intensified.

I saw the flames from the corner of my eye. They were bouncing on top of my skin, and before I could move my hand quick enough…

"Ouch!" he shrieked, and almost dropped me.

"What's wrong? Are you okay?"

His hand cupped his neck. "I think something bit me!"

"Let me see," I said.

He leaned down and took his hand away. A red welt the shape of a thumbprint sat just below his ear.

I gasped.

"What is it?" He asked, concerned.

"You're right," I replied, hiding my shock. "I think it's a bite. You should put some ice on it."

"Okay, I'll do that." He looked at me. "Are you okay? I didn't hurt you, did I?"

"No," I smiled, a little shy now "I'm good."

He put his hands on my waist, and gently pulled me to him again.

I turned my head to the side and gently pulled his hands off my waist. "It's getting late, I should get some sleep."

He stepped back and ran his fingers through his hair.

"Yeah, I should get back to my rounds."

I took a couple of steps and turned back but didn't know what to say, so I walked around the corner to my dorm. I stopped and leaned against the wall and held out my shaking hands' images of Rebecca's charred body were fresh in my mind. *Could I do to James what Cayden did to Rebecca?*

DOWNTOWN

I had a check-up at the hospital the next morning, which was just as well, as the first class of the day was Tactics with James. I was able to sleep in since I was still excused from morning runs. I tossed and turned all night. Images of James being charred to death by my touch wake me up in cold sweats.

Nurse Nina was on the shift this morning, and she smiled when she saw me.

"Oh, hi honey. Well, you look a lot better than the last time I saw you, that's for sure!"

I smiled back, "Yes, I'm feeling a million times better."

"You certainly gave everyone a good scare."

"I'm fortunate to have such good friends and surprised they would camp out when they could have been training, it is getting closer to graduation?"

"Didn't they tell you?"

"Tell me what?"

"It was that handsome instructor that led the way. He refused to leave until he knew you were better, so they all joined in.

"Oh," I said. "No, no one mentioned that part."

"Well, I expect he didn't want a fuss, or to put any stress on you. Speaking of that, let's check you out."

I went through the motions as Nurse Nina did her routine check-up, barely hearing what she said as she noted the results down. I felt even more horrible now. James stayed for me. He has no idea I could have burnt him to death.

"Angie, honey? Angie." Nurse Nina said.

"Huh? Oh sorry, just a lot on my mind."

"Well, that's understandable. Everything is looking pretty good, you're slightly pale, and your iron levels are a little low, so I suggest another week of light duties and adding a bit more extra meat and green veggies to your diet. I will give you some supplements to start you off."

"Okay," I said. "Come to think of it, I do feel like eating a burger."

"That's a good sign! Off you go, now." And before I could hop down from the bed, she gave me a big hug, which felt a little awkward at first, but her hair smelled like apple tree blossoms. Where had I smelled that before? It seemed so familiar. I hugged her back, just as hard.

I still had some time before lunch, so I sat on a bench outside the medic building. Jayla found me there.

"You're so lucky you didn't have Tactics this morning. James was in a real mood! Talk about waking up on the wrong side of the bed. Part of his neck was quite red, he kept rubbing it, maybe that was it, looked like he had been bitten or something.

I froze, and a fresh avalanche of guilt washed over me.

"He was not impressed when I asked about it, he made me do 30 more pressups. My arms are dead weights!" she said.

I didn't reply, and she looked up, rubbing her arms.

"What's up? Oh, was your check-up, okay? Did something happen?"

I couldn't look her in the eyes. "No, that was fine, well, except I'm slightly low on iron, but it's nothing a few burgers won't fix," I said. "Why didn't you tell me that James was the first one to stay at the hospital?"

"Well, there was so much going on at the time, and to be honest, I forgot. We were so worried about you."

We sat in silence for a bit, and then Jayla added, "He cares about you, Angie."

Before I could reply, a siren went off, blaring across the whole compound.

"What's that?" Jayla shouted.

"I think it's the call-to-action siren, we have to get to the hall!" And we took off at a sprint, down the hill.

We arrived at the hall, and all the other cadets were there, too.

"Any idea what's going on?" Mike said as he came up to us.

"No!" Jayla said, as subtle as ever, squeezing her hand into Mike's.

They didn't have to wait long before James arrived.

"Cadets," he said, "quickly, now, form up. The Police Commissioner has just briefed us himself. He needs everyone's support, and that includes all of you. The biggest Climate Change March in downtown Manhattan will be taking place this afternoon. We're not sure of the numbers, but over one million students have been given a free pass from school today if they have their parents' permission. It's a peaceful march, and our job is to keep it that way. Team Leaders, please come forward. I will brief you separately, and then you can go ahead and brief your detail. Each detail will be assigned a different area. The rest of you, go and eat a fast lunch and be back here in twenty minutes to suit up with equipment."

No one moved.

"Let's go, let's go, let's go, this is not a drill, people!" Everyone moved at once.

I headed towards James, along with Greg and Hamish, the other Team Leaders.

James was all business; our eyes locked briefly, but I couldn't read anything in them. My eyes flicked to his neck, which seemed quite swollen. Once given instructions, the others went off, and I lingered behind.

"James," I said.

"Not now, Whitewing. If it's nothing urgent, it can wait for the briefing at 1900 hours tonight."

"No, not urgent," I said, confused, as I hadn't heard of a briefing.

"Everyone suit up, and be on the buses in ten minutes!" James shouted.

We arrived in downtown Manhattan, and I couldn't believe my eyes. Every street was full of people, signs, and flags. Chanting and sirens filled the air.

My senses were lost by what was in front of me. Every emotion, all good and bad, and flashes of crime went through my head as people passed by me. My skin felt prickly and my mark was tender, I didn't see Cayden but thought he must be near.

I closed my eyes. *Get a grip! Focus on the job. You are a Police Cadet.* I took a deep breath and opened my eyes.

James directed each squad into position around the protest. "Remember," he said, "This is a peaceful protest. We are here to observe only but report if you see anything out of the ordinary."

Jayla stood next to me. "This vest is doing nothing for my figure!" she said.

I smiled.

"Woah," Jayla said, "Was that a smile?"

"Well, there's been a lot going on lately," I replied. Next to us, a teenage boy started to climb a lamppost, yelling, "I'd be at school if the planet was cool!"

"Something tells me this is about more than your collapse on the track," Jayla yelled over the increasing noise. More people had started to stream into the already crowded street.

"I don't think this is the time to talk about it," I yelled back at her.

Before Jayla could reply, there was a massive surge in the people. A huge wave of bodies came rolling toward us at full speed. I reached for Jayla's hand, but I was pushed far from the group. Separated from Jayla quickly, as they all chanted.

"What do we want? Planet justice! When do we want it? Now! What do we want? Planet justice! When do we want it? Now!"

The wave continued and got crowded, I tripped up out of nowhere and fell hard, brown boots stood stationary right beside my head but my tactics training came into practice immediately, and I went into a roll, my full uniform protecting me from the fall. But it was a forest of legs, and they weren't stopping, as if I was a hill to climb on and over. I grunted through each kick but rolled closer to the roadside as fast as possible. Almost there, the curb was ahead my mark started to burn and I knew something was wrong, a flame appeared in my palm this time it was different, it didn't appear out of practice it appeared as a warning that danger was near, then a big boot loomed over my head, and my last conscious thought was that looked like the same brown boots, before blacking out.

Something dripped on my head. I opened my eyes, confused, my head pounding. I tried to reach up to feel it but found that my hands were bound behind me. I looked around slowly. It was dark, and water dripped from the ceiling. Looking up,

I could see cracks of daylight, and realized I was in the old sewer tunnels.

Footsteps were coming towards me, so I pretended to still be unconscious.

"We should signal for Madam M," insisted a man's voice.

"Don't be stupid, she's busy. And you know what happened last time we called her for something that we should have dealt with ourselves," replied a female's nervous voice.

"Well, what are we going to do with her, then?"

"Find out what she knows, then get rid of her!"

Before I could react, a cold shock went through me as an icy bucket of water soaked me to the bone.

I gasped and if I had any advantage, I lost it when they dragged me to my feet, gurgling and sputtering out water.

"You awake then, beauty?" the man sneered at me.

I noticed my vest, radio, and taser had been taken off and were in a corner, too far away for me to reach.

"Who are you, and what do you want? I am a New York Police Cadet, and it is against the law to kidnap…" I looked up to face him to let him know I would not be afraid or bullied. My blood started to thump, but irregularly, like a wheel that had fallen off a wagon. There was nothing good to this man, but what was scary is that I wasn't even sure he was fully human, his features shifted, between man and beast but his intentions were clear, he was very happy to hurt me and do whatever it took to get what they wanted…whatever that was. Despite my brave face, I was so afraid I thought my heart might stop.

"Just get on with it," the woman said and punched me so hard my head rung. My lip started to gush with blood, the blow almost sending me unconscious again. I slid back to the ground.

"Stop, Bee, or she'll be dead before we get any information."

"Hmph," she said and crossed her arms.

A siren was blaring in my head, and spots danced around the front of one of my eyes. I couldn't open the other eye.

I focused on my breathing and turned my head slowly to them.

"Now let's start again, Miss New York Police Cadet," the man said, sarcastically.

"Tell us right now how you got that mark, and we will set you free."

"What mark?" I mumbled.

The woman—Bee was her name? —lifted her hand again, and I flinched. The man grabbed her arm, so quickly I didn't even see him move.

"I won't tell you again!" he yelled, and this time she stepped back without a word.

"Don't play dumb," he said to me. "The one on your palm."

"I don't know what you're talking about," I replied, sounding braver than I felt.

"Let me guess, you dug your claws into some high-ranking demon who fell in love with you. Being a Demon is a privilege, an honor and you have to earn it. You make me sick!".

He was at me so fast, his hands around my throat. The pressure was light, but the threat was there.

"You don't want to play with me, police girl. If you think that punch was hard, you haven't seen anything, yet." He started to increase the pressure on my throat. I began to gasp for air, and the spots returned.

But my fire started to swirl quickly to protect me I could feel it travel from my palm, up my arms through my rib cage to my throat, then I smelled burning flesh before he screamed.

"My hands, my hands!" Smoke was coming off them, and bits of flesh flew off as he frantically waved them around.

"Let me at her!" Bee demanded.

Before he could respond, I heard running footsteps, coming toward us.

"Not now, let's go! This isn't over." He spat at me. Bee grabbed a coat, wrapped it around his hands, and scrambled up the nearest ladder to the street.

"Stop, police!" shouted a familiar voice.

James ran in with some cadets behind him, but before he reached the ladder, they had already disappeared over the top. Daylight streamed down on top of me, and I blinked, blinded.

"Angie!" Jayla screamed as she ran to me.

James immediately turned in disbelief. His face ran through a mixture of emotions, but he quickly composed himself as his training kicked in.

"Quick, let's get her uncuffed. Reggie, call in the paramedics. Jayla, get water and a blanket."

"Angie, can you speak?" he asked as he uncuffed me, "Are you okay? Where does it hurt?"

The blood rushed back into my arms.

"I'm okay," I lied. "My head hurts, though. What took you guys so long?" I tried to smile but hissed from pain as my lip gushed again.

"I'm not waiting for the paramedics. Let's get you out of here." He scooped me up carefully.

"This is becoming a habit," I muttered, but relief spread through me, and I let my head fall against his shoulder. I dozed as he carried me back through the tunnels. Jayla put a blanket over me and insisted on holding my hand.

The paramedics were at the entrance. As soon as we came out, James put me down carefully on the stretcher. Around us, the streets were almost empty. Flags and rubbish were everywhere.

"The streets are still barricaded off after the protest. They will be reopened soon, so let's get you out of here," James said as if reading my thoughts. "Angie, what happened? Who did this?"

He looked like he wanted to hurt someone. My head was so sore. It was hard to concentrate, and forming the right words was a struggle.

"I… I don't know. I was tumbling in a wave of people, and something hit my head. When I came to, there was a woman and a man. She punched me hard, I refused to tell them anything, and…" The words slurred out slowly and tears started to fall. "The man put his hands around my throat, and he started to squeeze… I couldn't breathe, and that's when you came…"

"I think that's enough for now," the medic said, interrupting. "Your heart rate is going up, and I don't want you to pass out. You have a nasty bump to the head. It looks like you have a concussion, but you're lucky. Let's get you to the hospital for some monitoring."

They started to lift me into the ambulance, and Jayla came over quickly to hug me.

"You're the bravest person I know," she said, with tears in her eyes. "I'll come and see you as soon as we get back."

James stood back and nodded at her, and as the doors closed, his eyes clouded over with a rage I had never seen before.

COMMENDATION

Curled on my side, I stared at my bedside wall. It was full of pictures, and funny notes from Jayla who'd written them while she was bored in some class lecture. The camera had been a gift from my mother for my eighteenth birthday before she disappeared. The first thing I wanted to do, of course, was to take a photo of her, but she refused and said that instead, my heart will always choose the right pictures to remember when it needed to. I still don't know what she meant by that.

I smiled at a picture of Dad and me when I'd first joined the Academy. He had insisted on driving me up here, and to my surprise took some days off from work so we could explore the city together. There was a welcome orientation day for cadets and family, and I was thrilled he was there. I was so nervous! He had called me after what happened; the Academy had rung him straight away as protocol. He wanted to come to visit, but I told him I was okay. I had been released the same day, battered and bruised, and put on bed rest and light duties for a few days. My face ached, but more than that I was still pretty shaken up. I couldn't face the other cadets, not with this beat-up face. My hands wouldn't stop shaking, and the fire was back in my dreams, and I knew it was dangerous to ignore it because I could get fire fever, but I couldn't turn up, not yet. I hadn't seen James either. Jayla had been the only one around.

Right on cue, she bounced into the dorm.

"Hey girl, how are you feeling? Up to coming to lunch today?"

"I'm not hungry," I muttered, my back to her, still facing the wall.

"You've been here for two days; you can't hide forever. And besides, I'm not going to take no for an answer, and you know how annoying I can be. Please?" she said in a very whining tone.

I sighed and turned to her. "Look at me Jay, I'm a mess. No one wants to see this purple face. It's embarrassing."

Jayla softened. "You're wrong, Angie. Everyone cares about you, why can't you see that? Come to lunch please, or I'll sit here with you all day talking about Mike, and how delicious his lips are!"

I groaned. "No, anything but that!"

"They are delicious, you know."

"I'm up, I'm up," I said, putting my shoes on. "Just give me a minute."

While in the bathroom, I looked in the mirror. I could open my right eye now, but it was an explosion of colors, yellow and purple-black. My lip was still swollen; it needed a couple of stitches. I brushed and coiled up my hair with my shaky hands noticing the red streak had faded. *Just breathe, you can do this.*

We arrived at the mess hall, but I stopped before going in, rubbing my hands on my pants.

"It's lunch, Angie. Come on, I'm starving!"

We opened the doors to the mess hall. There were tables full of cadets, happy chatter, and wafts of delicious food.

Everyone stopped what they were doing and stared at me, and I froze, unsure of what to do.

Jayla looped her arm through mine and started to pull me forward.

Reggie started to clap, then Mike, and before I realized it, the whole hall was clapping and standing up. Tears came to my eyes, and Jayla beamed. We sat down at the nearest table with Reggie and Mike. The clapping just kept going, and I blushed.

James and the other instructors were there. He cupped his hands. "Settle down!" Slowly, the clapping stopped, and everyone took their seats. James still stood.

"Whitewing," he said, his face unreadable. "You sure know how to get attention!"

Everyone laughed, and I relaxed a little. He smiled then, a huge smile. He took a piece of paper out of his pocket. "Angela Mary Whitewing." I looked at Jay, who was still beaming.

"I, the Police Commissioner of the New York Police Department, would like to award you with a medal of valor, for acts of outstanding bravery. It is cadets like yourself that make my job easier. It is your bravery that keeps our streets safe and helps to build a better future for new generations. 'Thank you,' is not a big enough statement, but I hope you do accept this medal and wear it with pride."

Everyone erupted in applause. I winced again as Jay hugged me tightly.

I couldn't quite believe it. It took a while for everyone to settle down.

James said, "Angie, we know you are still healing from this, mentally and physically. You have shown great bravery and commitment, not only to your uniform but to yourself and your country. We are all in this together." He looked at everyone. "We train together, we fight together, and we heal together.

We are all here for you. I promise you we will catch who did this!"

The hall erupted again. It was deafening, and no one was going to stop it this time. Tears fell freely down my face.

I knew I should have rested that night, but once Jayla's snores started, I went out to the target training area, my fire insisting. I didn't know if Cayden would be there, but I would practice on my own if he wasn't. I wanted to see him though, and now that my concussion had lessened, the events of that day were coming back to me. This was no accident, and there were details I couldn't share with the Academy. Well, not yet, anyway.

It was dark out, apart from some lights through the compound. The wind was icy, and Winter was close, but with my fire, I could feel the wind on my skin. I was glowing inside.

I could see the target grounds from a distance, and my skin started to get prickly and my mark got warmer. I noticed that I could sense him from further away, now.

Cayden was sitting on the bench with his back to me, and I knew he could sense me too. It felt like I hadn't seen him for ages; this last week had taken its toll and made me doubt myself in every way possible. I felt like giving up, which was a first for me. I still couldn't believe what had happened at lunch. It felt like a dream, and I knew now that I needed to be here to see this through, to follow where this path led.

My fire started to swirl in excitement as I got closer.

Cayden turned around. "Hi, where have you…" He was at me so fast I didn't see him move, and he touched my cheek tenderly.

"What happened?" he asked with grave concern on his face. We hadn't been this close before, and for a moment, I couldn't respond confused by the intensity of my feelings, and I took a step back.

"Oh, this? You should have seen the other guy," I said, trying to make light of it. "But I don't know how to control these things." I held up my hands.

"What? Hang on, start at the beginning. Sit," James said, as he pointed at the bench.

I recounted the full events and teared up again at the choking part. Cayden's face seemed to grow more and more crimson as I went on.

"But what I didn't tell the Academy was that when I saw this man, it was like nothing I have seen before, Cayden. He, it—I'm still not sure what I saw. His features kept shifting, It was clear he was not good but it was horrifying almost as if it saw me too, some kind of beast but not attached to him. I'm scared Cayden, what if that 'thing' comes back for me? And how did I melt his hands? Am I a monster, will no one be able to touch me? I mean, it was good that he let me go, but I need to control my fire."

Cayden stood up. "And you said the woman's name is Bee?" he asked.

"Yes, I think so. Why?"

"I need to ask around. I think I know who they are. Well, I know someone who does."

"You do?" I asked, excited. "Let's go and get them now and bring them in—or better yet, I can give their location to James, and they can bring them in. I feel terrible about not giving them the full account of what happened."

"No, you don't understand. If my hunch is correct, you're fortunate. They weren't human."

"So, they're demons like us?"

"I have to go."

"But I need some training, Cayden. My fire is getting out of control."

"Just stay here and do some of the exercises I taught you. Meet me back here, same time tomorrow night."

And before I could respond, he left. I paced for a second I needed answers. I decided to follow him, I quickly ran in the direction he went but there was no sign of him, I approached the charred tree and I could feel the energy coming from it, I reached out to touch it and it started to glow and my hand went through. Scared but determined I shut my eyes and walked into the tree it must be some kind of portal.

In a second I was in a cold dark, damp hallway, and I could hear and feel a rumbling train going past on the other side of the wall. I wiped a drip off my forehead that had fallen from the ceiling. I opened up my palm and my mark illuminated and A flaming ball sprung up, steady and strong. I looked around, the tunnels looked unused, I had heard there were miles of tunnels under New York streets.

I heard a noise nearby and moved my hand towards the sound, I saw a door slightly ajar. I moved closer and could see Cayden.

My skin got prickly and my fireball grew brighter.

I peeked around the gap careful to stay in the shadows there were rows and rows of bookshelves. and deep purple velvet armchairs sat by an empty fireplace, with what looked like an animal basket nearby. Cayden walked up to the fireplace and opening his palm sent a purple flame into it.

Oh wow, he has to show me how to do that adding that to my mental list of things to learn.

Nothing happened at once, and Cayden started to pace around with clenched fists.

A huge snake appeared in the fireplace first, I covered my mouth so as not to call out to Cayden, was he in danger, do I need to go in? My palm started to glow in anticipation and the fire swirled ready beneath my skin. The snake hissed at him and just before I was ready to barge into the room, it coiled into the basket like a cat, I couldn't believe what I was seeing.

"Hate you too Kaia," Cayden said to the snake.

The snake hissed at him again.

More smoke appeared. And Cayden's mother stood outside of the fireplace.

"You rang, son? How lovely of you to request to see me. It's much more comfortable here than in that horrid and damp wooded area."

"It was you, wasn't it," he said through clenched teeth.

"I have no idea what you're talking about. Now, come. Sit with me." His mother said as she sat down in one of the velvet chairs.

"I will never forgive you for this. Tell me right now!" he shouted and slammed his fist on the table in front of her. Making me jump at the door, I had never seen him this angry before.

The snake rose and hissed at him.

"Did you send those vile creatures after Angela?"

"Oh, that's what has got you all ruffled? Well, you don't need to shout, don't be silly. I give them a sense of direction, and how they interpret that is their choice. Besides…" She turned serious and looked at him with her black eyes. "Your way is not working, and we needed to send a message to try and flush out Gavriel."

Did I hear that right? She's talking about my mother; she's looking for her too. Does that mean she is alive?! Tears formed in my eyes, there had always been a part of me that thought she was dead. I wiped my tears away and turned my attention back to Cayden.

"This is not your place," he said, barely containing his rage. "Do not interfere, and never use those creatures again. Do you hear me?"

"You no longer have command of this, my only son." She stood up and ran her nails along the snake's back, which made a rumbling hissing sound in delight.

"I have been asked to assist, by a higher order. So, you see, I will use whatever method I choose. Once Angela is out of that Academy, it will all be so much easier to reach her without being surrounded by humans all day and night," she said, smiling. "Until then, stay out of my way—professionally, of course, darling. But I would love to see you for dinner."

I saw Cayden clench his fists and turned around heading back towards me still furious.

I stepped back into the shadows, reached for the portal, and slipped back into the forest.

The forest was cool and calming, I popped my flame up, it felt good to let it loose.

My head was swirling, I wasn't sure whose side Cayden was on, it proved I couldn't trust him but now that I knew my mother was alive, I couldn't push him away, I had to know everything he knew and why Cayden's mother want me so much?

I walked back up the hill to bed, hopefully, some sleep will help.

SHAKEDOWN MONTH

A blaring alarm sounded through our dorm, waking us up.

"What the hell is that?" Jayla shrieked.

I looked at the time through blurry eyes it was 3 am, and I had only been back in bed a few hours.

"I don't know," I yelled back.

James' voice came over the speaker. "All cadets get dressed and get down to the hall immediately. You have five minutes!"

Jayla groaned. "What? I feel like I just went to bed."

"You did," I grinned back at her. "That will teach you for sneaking around with Mike.

I was lucky this time, Jayla returned to the dorm only 15 minutes after I had, I need to think of some excuses in case I get caught next time.

I yawned, 'Ok let's go!"

In the training hall, everyone still looked half asleep.

"Cadets," James said. "You're in the last month here." Everyone smiled and looked at each other.

"This last month is going to test all that you have learned. It's called a shakedown month." James walked along in front of us slowly, and you could feel the excitement radiating from him. "There will be midnight drills and unexpected inspections. You will need to be on your toes, alert, and work as a team. If one of you falters, the rest will go down. This is serious." James looked at Jayla and Mike, and to Jayla's credit, she blushed, but she stood a little taller.

"I'm proud of you all, but it's not over yet! You will be granted more freedoms." Everyone started to cheer. *"But,"* James said, holding up his hand. "This is also testing you, remember that. Your badge is part of who you are, so you need to act like it, even when you're not in uniform. Okay, any questions?"

Jayla put up her hand. "Can we go back to bed now?" I suppressed a laugh.

James sighed. "Ms. Price, did you hear anything I just said? No, you're all going to do drills for the next hour. Then if you're lucky you can go back to bed. Let's go, twenty push-ups, right now."

Jayla looked shocked, and I couldn't help but laugh.

"Come on, Jay, four weeks to go."

"This is so not happening!" she said, as she started her push-ups.

When we got back to our dorm, it was 4 a.m. Jayla did a belly flop on her bed, uniform and all, and started to snore.

I was just about to do the same but noticed a green card sitting on my pillow. Picking it up, it felt strange, and my skin started to prickle.

Angie, I enjoyed our evening together, more training tonight, same place. —Cx

I put it down, and suddenly it dissipated into a green cloud and disappeared.

Now, that was cool! He has to show me how to do that. I thought.

I was worried, though. With these drills and the unexpected change in routine, I didn't know if I could get out to see him without raising suspicion. I yawned, eyes closing. I was too tired to figure it out now. I threw off my boots and dove into bed.

The 5 a.m. alarm came around too fast.

"Make it stop!" Jayla's voice muffled as she threw a pillow over her head. "This is torture."

I was back to full duties today, so even though I was as tired as Jayla, I wanted to make the most of it. My face had turned all shades of yellow and green, but it was feeling much better.

"Let's go get breakfast," I said.

"Well look who is Miss Perky this morning. I need coffee," Jayla said as she slowly headed to the shower.

Everyone was standing around the notice board in the breakfast hall, chatting excitedly.

"Oh, everyone is too awake. I'm going to get coffee first," Jayla said, making her way to the front.

I went over to the crowd and edged my way forward. It was everyone's scheduled leave times. Now, this was exciting!

"Jayla," I shouted, "you're going to want to see this!"

Coffee in hand, she had some color on her face.

"Oh, yes!" she said, scanning the sheets. "Oh, wait. We don't have any time off together this week?"

I looked. She was right. "That's not the worse part, though," I said. "Neither do you and Mike."

"What? You've got to be kidding me!"

"Are you surprised, Jay? I mean, you guys haven't exactly kept it a secret."

She pulled a sad puppy dog face.

"Oh, come on, use that huge brain of yours, I'm sure you can find someone to swap with—unofficially, of course." I hated to see her so sad.

"You're a genius," she said. As if on cue, Mike and Reggie came through the doors.

Jayla bounced over to them and dragged them to the boards. I went to get some breakfast, and I could hear her planning and trying to convince Reggie to swap with her.

I sat down, lost in my thoughts, so I didn't even notice him sitting next to me.

"Earth to Angie," he said.

"Huh?" I looked up, and James looked at me, amused.

"You were so far away you didn't even notice I'd sat down. There go my instructions about being on alert," James teased.

"Oh, oops," I said blushing. James was so close I could smell his fresh aftershave and minty shampoo, his hair still slightly damp.

He laughed. "Did you see the leave schedule?"

"Yeah, I did. Jayla's not too happy."

"Well, no, surprise there. What's your first time?"

"I have this afternoon off."

"Want to grab a coffee?"

I blinked at him in surprise. "Um, is that allowed?" I whispered, suddenly aware of our conversation and who might be listening.

James laughed again. "Yes, of course. It's in our own free time, and we are out of uniform. You can turn me down, you know, but be gentle." He said it with some hurt in his voice, but he was still smiling and had a cheeky twinkle in his eyes.

"Sure, of course!" I said, a little too fast.

"Well, all right then. I'll meet you at D's Diner just around the corner at three."

And before I could reply, he left.

Wow, did that happen?

Jayla jumped in next to me with Mike and Reggie in tow.

"It's all sorted," she said excitedly. "I'm swapping with Reggie, which means Mike and I can go on an actual date this afternoon!" Mike was smiling, too; Reggie didn't look so excited.

"It's not like you gave me much choice," he grumbled. "I was going to see if Whitewing wanted to catch a movie."

"You were?" Jayla and I asked at the same time.

"Well, I don't want to go by myself and be a loser," he said, suddenly defensive.

"Oh, thanks, but maybe another time. I'm catching up with someone," I said.

"Wow that was quick," Jayla said. "Who is it?"

I panicked and said, "Just a friend from out of town." *Now, why didn't I tell her the truth?*

"So where are you guys going to go?" I asked, changing the subject.

"Mike is such a romantic. We're going to have a picnic!"

"Blurgh." Reggie pretended to throw up.

I laughed. "Okay, we better get to class." I got up to go.

Jayla jumped up, too. "I'll see you later, sweetie," she said to Mike, giving him a quick smooch.

Outside, Jayla said, "Okay, out with it. That was weird."

"What was?" I tried to play it down.

"You and Reggie!"

"Oh, that. Yeah, that is weird, right? I'm sure he just wanted to go to the movies with someone, it was probably nothing."

"Hmmmmm, I dunno. I like the guy, but from what I've seen, he doesn't ask something for nothing."

"Maybe…" I said.

"Hey Whitewing, wait up."

Reggie jogged up to us.

"Jayla, can I have a quick word with Angie?"

"Sure, no problem, I will see you both in class." Jayla gave me a little excited wink as she left.

"Let's sit down for a minute," Reggie said, indicating a bench.

"Reggie, you're making me nervous. What's going on?"

He rubbed his palms on his pants.

"This is awkward. I know we didn't get off to a great start, and that was my fault. I was jealous of you, and how you're so sure of yourself, and anyway, sorry, I'm rambling. My father has an event, and I wondered if you would be my date." He looked away, not wanting to catch my eye.

"Your dad? I asked, as in the Chief of police?' I smiled, wanting to make him squirm just a little.

"Yeah," he said looking at his shoes.

"Of course, Reggie, if it means that much to you. I know we didn't get off to a great start, but I value your friendship. I hope you know that that's as far as it will go, though."

He laughed, then laughed some more until tears came to his eyes.

"What's so funny?" I demanded.

"Oh… you… thought…" In between gasps for air, he finally said, "sorry to disappoint, but I prefer the opposite sex."

"Huh?" I said, confused.

"I like men, Angie. That's another reason I was so spiteful of you—I liked James, and I could tell he has the hots for you."

I just stared at him in shock.

"Oh," I said, eventually. "Does anyone else know?"

"My closest friends know and I'm pretty sure my mother does, but I haven't told my parents directly, my father will take it the hardest. I would appreciate it if you don't tell them, please. That's why I wanted to ask you to come with me. He thinks you're the brightest star in the sky right now, so would think it's amazing if you did come…and for once, be impressed by me."

"But you have to tell them, Reggie. They would support you. We support you." I put my hand on his.

"I know you and the team here do," he said, sadly, "but Angie, please, I can't. This would crush my father," he said, sadly.

I felt terrible for Reggie.

"Okay, well I'm going to be the best date you've ever had, just watch me!"

Reggie perked up. "Really?"

"There is one thing, though."

"What is it? Anything."

"You're going to come shopping with me for a dress because I have no idea where to go."

"Deal," he said, smiling.

Reggie hugged me, and then we both hurried off to class.

After class, my free time started, and I was exhausted. So, I headed up to my dorm for a quick nap before going to meet James. There was a postcard from Dad waiting for me. He had won a big case and had taken a well-deserved vacation to Florida, before taking a road trip back to New York for my Graduation. He had rung beforehand, worried that he shouldn't go with my collapse and then the kidnapping, but I reassured him and he had gone. I was glad he was having a vacation and hopefully meeting some new people. We both felt Mom's absence, and I felt guilty that he was by himself. At least here, I had everyone.

I woke up in fright and looked at the clock. Yikes, 2:30? So much for a small nap!

I jumped up and threw on my best jeans, pulled my bun from my hair, it was so long now, and my red streak also seemed to be wider it was thicker and fuller and sat bright across my temple, but that could just be my imagination. I noticed just as I opened the door to leave that there was another green card from Cayden, this time on my dresser by the window, but there was no time to read it, now, I shoved it into my bag wondering why he had sent another so soon, did something happen?

THE LUNCH DATE

I stepped through the academy gates, there was a path that led past a busy highway road, it was always full of runners, and cyclists. Cayden's card was in my mind but I couldn't pull it out in such a public space. The diner was a ten-minute walk away and, at that time, I had started to imagine something was wrong, what if I was in danger? and when I arrived, I was a ball of nerves and jumpy wondering if his mother would try to ambush me out on the street.

The diner was bright and cheerful inside with vivid red leather seats. A jukebox was playing one of Mom and Dad's favorite songs, "All I Want to Do is Make Love to You," and I couldn't help but feel a pang of sadness. They loved those cheesy nineties love songs; they used to dance in the lounge with their old record player going. I used to tell them how gross it was, but in truth, I loved seeing them like that. I sighed and looked around. James wasn't here yet, so I grabbed the nearest booth. A waitress in a red frilly dress and a white apron came by and gave me a menu. It all looked delicious, and I realized I was hungry again.

"Hey, Sunshine," James said as he slid into the booth seat opposite me.

I realized that I hadn't seen him out of uniform. He was wearing crisp blue jeans and a simple long-sleeve tight-knit sweater, his arms bulged beneath his top—those arms that had saved and held me so many times.

"What looks good?" he said, picking up the menu.

You, I thought, but instead, I said, "I'm thinking of a burger, fries, and a chocolate milkshake."

He laughed, "Is that it?"

"Well, I could always order more if…" Then I realized he was teasing. "A girl has to eat too, you know. I'm still building up my energy."

James' face softened. He put his menu down and grabbed my hands. "Angie, I'm sorry. The other day was all my fault. I should never have split the teams up. I wanted to resign, but my commander wouldn't hear of it. Do you hate me? I understand if you do."

For the second time that day, I was in shock from what I'd heard. I just stared at him.

The waitress came back over to take our orders, and James took his hands off mine. I mumbled out what I wanted, not even realizing that my lips had moved.

When she had left, I said, "What are you talking about? The kidnapping wasn't your fault. You tried to resign, and turn in your badge? But this means more to you than anything, and everyone loves you!"

"I couldn't bear to think of someone hurting you. It took all my strength not to prowl the streets on my own to hunt for whoever did that to you," he said with hate in his eyes.

"Don't be that person, James. Don't be hateful. Yes, it was awful, and I'm still recovering in many ways, but don't let this rule your life. I'm okay. I'm still here." I smiled at him and took his hands.

We were jolted out of our moment by a massive bang on our booth's window; we both looked up but saw nothing.

"Maybe a bird?" James said, shrugging.

But across the street, I saw Cayden. *Oh no, it must be bad if he's here.*

"Um, I just have to go to the girl's room. I'll be right back, don't drink my milkshake when it comes, okay?"

He grinned. "Well, you better be quick then."

There was a window in the girl's toilets, which I opened. Cayden was there, and my skin prickled and flames swirled beneath in greeting.

"What's going on Cayden?" I asked in a whisper.

"I might ask you the same thing. What are you doing out, and aren't you both looking cozy? Did you burn his flesh yet?"

"What? Oh really, that's how it's going to be? Okay, goodbye Cayden!"

"Okay, sorry, I didn't mean it. I need to talk to you, and you have ignored my demongram."

"The what, now?"

"The green cards."

"That's what it's called? Okay, that's cheesy. Can't you just text or something?"

"No, I can't, or I would have, all right?"

"I didn't ignore them, I got one from last night and I have your other one in my bag, I was going to read it as soon as I could, I swear".

"This is serious Angie, are you going to spend all of your time with lover boy, or are you going to take your training and what just happened to you seriously?"

"What's gotten into you? The routines have changed, and in the last four weeks we've had random drills at all hours, and I just can't predict what I will need to do. I can't risk it, there are only four weeks left of the program.

But I do get some leave where we are allowed to leave the Academy for a few hours, on allocated days. The next one is the day after tomorrow at 3 p.m. Do you want to meet here?"

"Okay, if I must. This place is a bit rougher around the edges than I'm used to."

"I'm sure you'll survive. Goodbye, Cayden." I shut the window.

Back at the table, our order had arrived.

"Good to see you didn't drink my milkshake," I said.

"Well, I did consider it," James replied, "but I ordered one for myself, instead." He pointed to the already empty glass.

"That was quick," I laughed as I sucked on my milkshake straw.

A slightly awkward silence settled between us. I wanted to talk about that night but didn't know where to begin. I stuffed my mouth with burgers and fries in the hope he would start first.

"Do you think you should order another one?" James laughed.

I looked down, and he was right; the burger was already gone.

"I told you I was hungry," I said, wiping my mouth with my napkin.

"I also wanted to apologize for the other night… I hope I wasn't too rough…" He trailed off.

"No, it was my fault. I got a bit carried away, and I think I freaked out a little. Sorry for running off. I didn't want to stop," I said, blushing.

James nodded and smiled, but his eyes didn't reflect the warmth.

"That's one of the reasons I wanted to meet with you today. I think while things are intense over the next four weeks, it's probably best if we keep it professional between us."

My mouth dropped. "Now you want to keep it professional?"

"Don't be like that Angie," he said, reaching for my hand. I pulled further away from him.

I grabbed my coat. "Wow, you know how to treat a girl. I think you need some more practice at this dating thing. You can at least get the bill. And don't worry, I will be very *professional;* your reputation is safe!" I stormed out of the Diner while the jukebox sang, "I Will Always Love You," by Whitney Houston.

GOODBYE

I went for a run to clear my head and completely forgot about the demongram. I could see my breath in the icy air; the sun was setting earlier, with winter around the corner. Who did James think he was? He was the one that came onto *me*—I was keeping it professional! What a waste of my first afternoon out; I could have gone to see a movie with Reggie after all.

After only two miles, breathing became difficult. I knew I should stop; this was my first run since the kidnapping, and I didn't want to push it. I needed to work on getting my fitness back up.

Back at our dorm that night, I was still fuming when Jayla came in.

"What's up with you? Did you see your friend from out of town?" Jayla asked.

I had forgotten about that. "Oh, no. He was a no-show."

"Well, no wonder you're all sulky."

Jayla stood in front of me, grinning.

"What?" I asked.

"Go on, ask me."

I stared at her blankly.

"My date!" Jayla said, bouncing up and down.

"Oh, sorry, Jay! How was your first date?"

She leaped onto the bed next to me. "It was so romantic! We went for a walk around the lake at Central Park. It's so beautiful this time of year, because all the trees are golden, and their leaves make blankets on the paths. I don't know how Mike did it, but he had a blanket and a basket full of the yummiest things. We just sat there all afternoon."

"I'm so happy for you, Jay." I hugged her and it cheered me up, just a little.

"I've been dying to ask, what did Reggie want?"

"I'm sure he won't mind me telling you, and besides, I need your help, too."

"Out with it!" Jayla said jiggling up and down.

"His dad is holding this ball-gathering, and he wants me to be his date."

"*Wow!*" Jayla got up off the bed.

"It's not a big deal," I said.

"Are you kidding? It's the Police Commissioner's Ball, Angie!"

I stared at her blankly again.

"You know, the most influential party of the year? Even my parents are going!"

"Oh," I said quietly, freaking out. "Maybe I shouldn't go. I don't need any more pressure, at the moment."

"You have to go now. What are you going to wear?"

"Well, that's the thing I was going to ask you for your help with. Reggie is going to come with me too, but I need you. Can you come and help me pick something?"

"Yes, I would love to. I would be insulted if you *didn't* take me."

"Thanks! I'm nervous now. I just wanted to help Reggie out."

"Don't be, it will be great. We'll find you the right dress; you'll see. I'll do your hair and makeup, and you will be the belle of the ball!"

I smiled weakly at Jay's enthusiasm. *What have I gotten myself into?*

As it turned out, the only day we could all get off together to find a dress was the day I was supposed to meet with Cayden. Mike had to swap with Jayla to give her the slot, and he wasn't too happy about not spending that time with her. However, when Reggie bravely came out to them and explained his reasons for needing the help, they understood and were in total support.

I texted Cayden that I couldn't make it, and said I was going shopping for an important dress. I still didn't know how to make those demon card things; what were they called, again? I hoped he got my text because he didn't reply.

Reggie, Jayla, and I waited just outside the security gates. A shiny black limo rolled up.

"Woah!" Jayla said.

"Is this for us?" I asked, smiling. "I have never been in a limo before."

"Sure is. My dad is excited that you can come, and so am I, so we may as well enjoy ourselves a little, for once!"

"Eeek, let's go," Jayla said and jumped into the door the driver held open for them.

The limo headed towards downtown Manhattan and stopped along Fifth Avenue. We all jumped out, and Jayla looked windswept from insisting the driver open the sunroof, so she could stand up in it the whole way. I laughed at her as she patted down her hair.

I truly felt like I was in *Pretty Woman*. The soundtrack was playing in my head as we leaped from shop to shop. Nothing took my fancy, but Jayla wanted them all. Time was running out and I was tired. I hoped this was the last shop. From the outside, it looked too fancy, and definitely out of my price range, but Reggie insisted that we came in. After trying on ten different dresses, even Jay was looking tired. I finally strutted out with the last one on. Reggie and Jay both sat straight up and looked at each other.

"Please say that this is the one," I said. "I know it's a bit unusual, but it feels right, somehow."

Jayla stood up and twirled me around. "You look stunning, Angie! It looks like the material is moving around you."

I looked into the full-length mirror. The dress had three layers of material, but it was an illusion, as it appeared to be one piece. There was a black satin layer that hugged my body and held my shape. There was also a vibrant red shimmery material that was on top, but looser, with bright shoulder straps. The very top layer of white flowed down, embracing the other two colors, and bringing them together. The overall effect was mesmerizing.

Reggie stood up too. "Wow, Angie, where have you been hiding that body?"

They all laughed. I said, "Have you seen the price tag? Yikes!"

"I got this, don't worry," Reggie said.

"No way," I said, "You can't."

"Don't sweat it. What's the point of a credit card with no limit on it if I never use it?"

They all smiled.

"Well, I'm starving," Jayla said. "Can the credit card cope with a late lunch, too?"

"I think it will manage. We'd better head back to the Academy, after that."

When I got back to the dorm with my giant box, there was another demogram waiting on my pillow I felt suddenly guilty that I had completely forgotten about the other one, I opened up my bag but it had disappeared. Jayla had headed off to see Mike before dinner so I was finally alone.

I picked it up, and my blood started to pump as I felt that strange sensation again, like I was reaching into another dimension.

Don't ever text me, it's not safe. You have to risk coming out tonight, it's IMPORTANT. —Cx.

As soon as I put it down, it dissipated into a green cloud and disappeared.

I was still angry with James, but at least Cayden wanted to see me. My fire missed him too, so I would have to risk it. Plus, I needed to confront him about what I heard the other night.

I decided to sneak out earlier, as the drills tended to be between midnight and 2 a.m. I told Jayla I was going to bed early, and since she didn't want to disturb me, she decided to do the same. So, at 10:30 p.m., when her light snores started, I rushed out.

Cayden wasn't there. I worried the earlier time might have thrown him off, and I couldn't text him, so I sat for a while, practicing my flame ball and wondering how I could make a message out of it. I had created a flame-shaped rectangle when Cayden appeared.

"Looks like you've been practicing," he said, Good of you to be able to make the time to take your life or death seriously" he added sarcastically.

"Look, I'm sorry, okay? It's not like it's my fault, I'm trying to finish training for my career, it's important to me. I want to be a detective so I can look into my mom's disappearance.

"Speaking of your mother…" Cayden sat down next to me, opened up his palm, and a green ball appeared.

Distracted, I said, "Why is your flame green, and how do you make those demongrams"

"Did you hear me, Angie? I need to talk to you about your mother."

I closed my palm immediately, and my flame disappeared.

"I followed you Cayden, the other night, I followed you to your mothers' underground library, I wanted to see if you would tell me.

"Angie, I don't know where she is"

"But you knew she is alive, you lied to me" I stood up angry

"Angie, sit. Please don't overreact."

"Overreact? You knew how hard I have been training, how much I want to find her, and you tell me not to overreact? Tell me what you know Cayden"

"I don't know anything, Angie." He threw up his hands in defense. "I don't. But I do know she's alive; that's what I have been trying to tell you. Those creatures that kidnapped you were a setup from my mother, and I had no idea she had planned it."

"What are you talking about? What has that got to do with my mom?"

"My mother wants to put you in danger so that your mother will come out of hiding. Those creatures are demon slaves. They give part of their human soul in exchange for demonic powers, so that's why you couldn't see into them fully, and their appearance kept shifting. They hope that if they do their demon master's bidding, their master will complete the transformation and they will be demons with powers of their own. But so far, this has never happened. It takes a powerful demon to make these creatures, as it is, but only a mighty demon can fully convert them; even my mother isn't strong enough, but they don't know this, so they continue to do her bidding out of hope."

"But why would your mother want *my* mother? She wouldn't hurt a fly.

I sat down next to Cayden rubbed my face with my hands and turned to him.

'Cayden is my mother a Demon? Is that why your mother wants her? Is she a powerful demon and she is needed to finish the transformation of those horrible creatures?

Cayden put his hand on mine. "I wish I had the answers you need".

"You must know more! I don't believe that you're telling me everything."

"The truth is I was initially sent to get close to you and find out if you knew where your mother was, and, if you didn't know, I was to use you to make her come out of hiding."

"This was all an act then?" I wasn't angry anymore; I was upset.

"No! I…well to start with, yes, but when you came back to the prison, I knew you were hurting, and after what happened with Rebecca and being in Prison it felt good to have someone care about what was going to happen to me. I went along with my mother's plans, so she wouldn't do anything like that stunt she'd pulled. Last week, I told her I don't want to be a part of it anymore, and that we are not pawns in her game." Cayden squeezed my hand.

"Angel, I care for you, I do. You have to believe me. I can feel it in my blood, I know you feel it too. Look, at my flames, can you see how happy they are? They love being close to you."

I wanted nothing more than for Cayden to put his arms around me and tell me that everything was going to be okay and that we could be together. My blood purred happily at his touch. Inside, my fire was happy, too. But I couldn't do it. I pushed his hand aside.

"I can't trust you, Cayden. I know none of this was your fault, but you knew, and you even went along with it. I can never forgive you for that." I stood up "I don't want to see you again. Goodbye, Cayden." I turned just as tears fell down my cheeks.

"But you don't understand, it's not safe."

"I can look after myself," I said as I walked up the hill, back to the Academy.

My blood and fire cried, and I felt a chill go across my skin

I will find my mother on my own.

THE BALL

I pumped up my running and fitness training big time; any spare time or afternoons I had I was running, boxing, or at the gym. I was determined to get through training at top fitness, and I wanted to be in top shape to take on whatever I might be assigned to next. I didn't know how I was going to find my mother now but if I was to take on other demons, I needed to be ready. I still couldn't believe Cayden he hides knowing my mother was alive and maybe a demon then wants us to be together!

I jumped out of the shower, three weeks to go 'til graduation, and now it was time to get ready for the Police Ball.

Jayla had kindly agreed to do my makeup. This was a first for me, and I wasn't the best at sitting still.

"Stay still Angie, or I'll end up poking your eye out," she said. "Didn't you go to a prom at school?"

"Nah, wasn't my scene. Ow!"

"I did say stay still. Your eye is watering now—let me fix your mascara."

"Are we almost done?"

"Yes, just your lips. I told my parents you're coming, so look out for them. They're nice, so if you need a comfort zone, use them, okay?"

"Thanks, Jay, that was nice of you."

"Okay, hold your lips at a pucker like this." She puckered up her lips, and I laughed.

"What?" she asked, grinning. "That's how it's done. Okay, just hold still, there. Okay, phew, done. Check out my amazing work in the mirror."

I turned around and was speechless. My eyes welled up.

"Oh no you don't; don't you dare wreck my masterpiece now!"

"Wow Jay, you're amazing. You should think about a career change."

"I'm just working with you, Angie. You're beautiful you know."

I gave her a huge hug. "Thank you."

"Okay, that's enough of that," she said, her eyes also welling up. "I'm sure Reggie and the limo are waiting."

She was right—I went downstairs and Reggie was there, ready to go.

"Wow! Is that you, White Wing?"

"You look very handsome yourself, Reggie."

"It took me so long to polish my shoes, but I knew my father would notice those first," he said. "Do my pants look too tight?" He did a little spin, grinning.

I laughed. "The dress uniform suits you. Wow, your shoes are crazy shiny; I can see my reflection. You have to give me some tips on doing mine before graduation."

He smiled. "Let's go, the limo is here." He held his arm out.

We arrived at the Police Commissioner's house. Many limos and expensive cars were dropping off people.

"Ready?" Reggie asked.

I took a deep breath. "Yes, I am."

Reggie hopped out first and offered his arm.

There were photographers at the ready, taking pictures, and there was even a little red carpet to guide people in.

"Is it always like this?" I asked, shielding my eyes from all of the flashes going off.

"Yes. It's only the elite families in society who come to this. And for some, it's the only event they go to so it's a rare opportunity for the press to get their pictures. It's also a charity event and a way for my father to keep the peace and show his support."

We walked through the white-columned entrance. A beautiful hall with a spiral staircase cascaded down. A sparkling chandelier hung from the ceiling, light bouncing off it in all directions.

"This place is really old. It's been handed down from one police commissioner to the next. We live in a back wing—this is the formal entrance for guests and events."

"It's beautiful," I said, as I gazed up at the chandelier.

"May I take your coat, madam?" a doorman asked. He looked very dashing, clad in a matching top and trousers with red stripes down the sides, and white gloves on.

"Oh yes, thank you."

We walked through the entrance corridor, down a carpeted hallway with portraits hung on each side.

"These are all of the previous Police Commissioners," Reggie said.

We neared the end. Reggie pointed at the last portrait, and I couldn't help noticing the resemblance.

"That's my grandfather. I wanted to join because of him. Sometimes, when I was little, he would take me to work with him and take me out with him on jobs. I got to see first-hand the good and the bad, but also how each person can make a difference. He knew that I was gay, but he didn't care. We were going to tell my father together, but then he was killed in action five years ago."

"I'm so sorry, Reggie," I said, grabbing his hand.

"I felt so angry for a long time. Then I decided to join was the best way to channel that anger, and maybe make a difference."

"He would have been so proud."

Reggie nodded his head. "After he died, Dad and I drifted even further apart. He was surprised when I decided to join, he didn't think I had the stamina for it. He isn't exactly encouraging. It doesn't worry me—I want to do this for myself and my granddad—but I wish he was more supportive."

"Come on," I said, "let's go show him just how amazing you are."

Hand in hand we walked down the corridor, and we could hear piano music mixed with talking. We entered a beautiful ballroom with more stairs leading to balconies on either side, and rooms joining off to the back with a bar. Servers were holding silver trays of champagne by the glass. Reggie took two and handed me one.

"To you," Reggie said, clinking my glass. "Thank you for coming."

"I wouldn't have missed it for the world," I said and realized I meant that. Reggie had opened up to me and I was so grateful that I could do something to help him.

The ballroom was already half full, and people were in groups chatting amongst themselves. The piano music was soothing, and because of that and the sip of champagne, I was feeling relaxed.

I had linked arms happily with Reggie, my dress swishing across the floor as I walked.

My fire started swirling and I almost dropped my glass.

"Are you okay?" Reggie asked, looking at me with concern.

"Oh, yes," I lied. "Just not used to walking in these heels."

Reggie laughed. "Fair enough. We only have to make it over to the other side where my mother and father are. I want to introduce you."

I nodded and scanned the room; my fire swirling like this meant Cayden was close by.

As we approached the group, a woman broke off and ran to us immediately.

"Oh, Reggie Darling," she said and gave Reggie a huge hug.

"Hi, Mother," he smiled.

"You're so handsome, look at you!" she beamed.

"Mother, I would like to introduce Angela Whitewing." Reggie indicated to me our arms were still linked.

"Lovely to meet you, Angela. I have heard all about your unfortunate incident, and how brave you are. And you are so very beautiful, I must say." Then to my surprise, she hugged me.

"Mother is a hugger," Reggie said, as he laughed at the look on my face.

"Come, your father has to see how handsome you look in your uniform. Henry, look who's here!"

Reggie's father turned around and stepped out of the group but it wasn't him whom I saw instantly—not only was Cayden here but his mother which would have been enough for me to leave right there and then but to make it worse, James was also in the group and with a beautiful brunette that I didn't know, their arms linked. My blood thumped hard in my ears and I saw James and Cayden looking as shocked as I was. I felt my cheeks redden. Luckily Reggie's dad came right up to me to give me time to regain my composure.

"You must be Angela. Thank you for coming," The Police Commissioner said, shaking my hand.

He had the same mouth as Reggie, but the rest of his features were different: he was a bit shorter, and—despite being lean—had broad shoulders. His hair was greying at the temples, and his eyes were grey in color. I couldn't resist looking into him.

He wasn't a saint, but I could see that he genuinely thought the decisions he made would benefit his city, if not the country. He was ambitious and proud, and he did love Reggie. He thought being strict would give him the space and aspiration to succeed.

"I wouldn't miss it for the world commissioner. It's an honor to be here with Reggie. He is such a valued member of the cadets." I beamed at Reggie and pulled him next to me.

Reggie's mother smiled, and I saw a slight proud glint in his father's eye before he looked at Reggie. "It's good to see your shoes are polished correctly, son," he said before he moved off to introduce us to the rest of the group. Reggie rolled his eyes at his back.

The Commissioner indicated to James, "You, of course, know your instructor, James. This is his lovely girlfriend, Belinda."

Girlfriend? I internally sucked in my breath and managed a smile at Belinda. I shook her hand, and my birthmark stung. I held back a gasp.

"Nice to finally meet you, Angela. James speaks very highly of you."

I couldn't reply at first; my birthmark was still throbbing. I finally managed to blurt out, "Thank you, that is very kind."

The Commissioner continued his introductions. "I would also like you to meet Mrs. Montgomery and Cayden Montgomery."

I knew I couldn't avoid them—my blood was pumping like mad with them both here, and my fire rejoiced at being close to Cayden. Mrs. Montgomery didn't disappoint; she was wearing a purple satin dress with a high-laced collar up her neck. Long red satin gloves covered most of her arms, and her hair, which was tied into a complex bun, had a long snake brooch entwined within it. The snake rose its head and gave me a wink, and I knew it was her horrid snake in hiding. I bit my tongue, my hands itching to let my flame ball out.

"We know Angela well, Commissioner. Her father has been a great help to my family."

James, who still had a shocked expression on his face, blurted out, "You look stunning Angie."

Keeping my guarded smile firmly in place, I said, "Thank you, James."

The Commissioner continued his conversation, which I was glad for, stopping any further comments from James. "The Montgomery family has been a huge support to the Police Division and this city for the last decade, we couldn't do what we do without their charitable donations."

I smiled at this the best I could.

The band started to play. It was a classical band with a woman standing at a microphone in a gorgeous red sequined dress. She had a soulful voice, and for a few seconds, I was lost in her lyrics.

Reggie took my hand. "Would you do the honor of dancing with me?"

"That would be lovely." I let him lead me to the dance floor, three pairs of eyes following my every move. *Let them look.* I refused to be involved in whatever games they wanted to play anymore, but seeing James with someone was hurtful, had they been together the whole time? I felt like such a fool!

"You care for him, don't you?" Reggie asked, gently. I hadn't masked my face fast enough.

"Yes," I said. "I do, but I'm done." I stared up at him, determined. "I started this journey on my own, and I'm going to finish it my way."

"You know, Whitewing, you can be scary when you want to be." Reggie smiled at me.

"Thank you for being here. I appreciate you."

"Thank you, Reggie." I cuddled with him while we danced. "That means a lot."

Reggie murmured, "When you feel like sharing, I'm here for you too. I can keep secrets, and judging from your paparazzi over there, I'm sure you could use a friend."

"Oh, you noticed that, did you?" I murmured back into his chest.

"I think some plebe off the street would have noticed, let alone freshly trained Police Academy recruit Angie."

"Noted, thanks. But I got this for now. I might go and get some air though."

Reggie nodded. "I'll be over by the bar."

I stepped out into one of the many small balconies that surrounded the hall, inhaling deeply. It was a clear night; the stars twinkled overhead, and below I could see some latecomers' limousines still arriving.

Despite my brave face in front of Reggie I was starting to feel defeated, everyone I start to get close to either betrayed me or gives me half-truths, I didn't know what to believe anymore.

My fire started to swirl and I could feel my palm heating up, I didn't want to face Cayden right now, but when I turned around it was Belinda who sauntered onto the balcony. At first look, she was stunning—a bit too thin, long legs, long wavy dark brown hair—but upon closer inspection, her face was worn, mean.

My blood stirred, irritated, and I immediately went on the defense.

"Can I help you with something?" I asked, not succeeding at keeping an edge out of my voice.

"Come now, no need to be bitchy. I think we should try to be friends …"

She stepped towards me, my fire starting to swirl in alarm and my birthmark started to glow at the ready.

"After all," she continued, "we never got to finish getting to know each other." She stepped closer. She was taller than me and reached down to stroke my face. "I hardly recognized you. I think I prefer your face with blood and bruises."

I pushed her back, and my palm came up immediately with a fireball. "Who are you?"

"You don't know? Look at me properly, Angel."

Shocked and suddenly angry, my fireball grew bigger. "You have no right to call me that." And looking into her eyes, I realized instantly as her features kept shifting around what she was. I felt a chill and my ball of fire flickered. "It's you," I whispered. "From the sewers."

She clapped slowly, sarcastically. "Ahhh, she finally catches up. I don't think you're as smart as everyone says you are." She stepped forward again.

"Don't you dare come near me?" My flame ball grew again but I was afraid to let it go bigger than the size of my hand in case anyone saw us, my blood thumped in my ears, willing the flame to be let go.

"Or you will do what?" She reached out faster than I could see, and instantly squashed my flame ball between her fingers.

"As I was saying, I think we should be friends. We do have a love interest in common; why don't you join us?" She smiled at me and held out her hand. "I can show you how to use your powers."

A flame ball of her own appeared. It was purple and formed into a flat oval. "You can use your powers to convince people and manipulate them to your will." An image of James appeared, then my mother inside her purple flame.

Shocked I asked, "Do you know where my mother is?"

"Maybe, why don't you join us and I will answer any questions you have."

I seriously considered it for a second realizing she was trying to manipulate me now. Angry, I said, "I will never join you, whatever you are."

"Pity. Your mother will be so disappointed," she said as she turned to leave.

"What do you know about my mother?"

Before she could answer, Cayden walked in. He looked between us. "What's going on?" he asked.

"It's her, Cayden," I said, annoyed at the quiver in my voice.

"What do you mean Angie?" he asked, confused.

I looked around for an escape, estimating we were about two meters off the ground. I took a step back.

"From the sewers Cayden, it was her, she's a Demon Slave."

Cayden spun around to Belinda, "I'm sure you're mistaken Angie, Belinda is a Demon yes but she is no slave and I'm sure wouldn't have been one of those vile creatures from the sewers."

"Cayden you have to believe me, why would I lie about this?" My back was now against the banister.

A green fireball popped up on his palm and pointed it directly into Belinda's face. Her skin shifted in the eerie glow.

"Well, so she is," Cayden said, curiously.

"Get that thing out of my face," Belinda said as she smothered his palm with her hand. "And you can stay out of my way. I was having a lovely chat with Angel here." She smirked at me like a cat who just got its cream.

At the mention of my nickname, my palms immediately felt hot, and the fire was right at my fingertips. "You don't get to call me that."

"Oh really? Shall we see what happens if I say it again?" She took another step forward. "Ang …"

At that moment Reggie stepped out onto the balcony.

"Oh, here you are …" He started but stopped at the look on my face.

Worried for Reggie's safety, I stepped away from the balcony. Belinda didn't budge.

"Move, or be moved," I hissed between clenched teeth She hesitated but moved aside.

"Angie?" Cayden asked as I looped my arms with Reggie.

"I'm not interested, Cayden," I said, stepping back into the ballroom.

The orchestra music in full swing already started calming me.

"What was that all about?" Reggie asked.

"How well do you know Belinda?" I asked back.

"James' girlfriend?"

I swallowed a lump in my throat. "Yes … his girlfriend."

"I don't know her very well. I think they have been

on and off for a while. I think she works for Mrs. Montgomery, so that's how they met. They have been doing business with my father. I've met her only a couple of times, and she seemed okay. How did you two become enemies so fast?"

"What do you mean?"

"The air was sparking with energy between you two."

"Do you want to get out of here?" I asked quickly, spinning him around.

"Yeah, I guess so. I've done all the formal stuff I had to do; no one will notice now if I'm not here, but I'll just give my mother a quick goodbye. I will meet you at the entrance."

He let go of my arm and wandered back towards the group around his father and mother.

I couldn't stand to stay a moment longer, so I started to make my way through the ballroom, which was now full of dancers and people mingling. The sound of stringed instruments filled the air.

I nodded at a few people I recognized as I went through.

Before I got to the corridor a piano started up, and I instantly got goosebumps.

I turned around, and the same beautiful dark-skinned singer was sitting at a piano, playing and singing "Everything I Do, I Do It for You," another one of mother's favorite songs. I was mesmerized and stood there watching her my eyes welling up. *I hope you're okay, Mom.*

"She's great, isn't she?" Reggie asked, pulling me from my thoughts.

"Who?"

"The singer. She does a lot of the functions here."

"Oh yes. The song she was playing was one of my mother's favorites."

"Still want to go?" He asked.

"Oh yes, please."

We started down the corridor past the portraits.

"You never talk about her."

I didn't reply, just shrugged.

"Your mother—you said it was one of her favorite songs, so I'm assuming she isn't around anymore?"

I stopped at the portrait of Reggie's grandfather.

"No, your right I should talk about her more?"

"No pressure," he said kindly but waited.

Tears welled up in my eyes "Just like your family is the reason why you wanted to be a Police officer, my mother is also my reason. One day she just disappeared and we haven't seen her since, we all searched everywhere and I put up posters and nothing, I joined the Academy thinking once I'm trained, I will have better resources and ideas to help me find her, but I'm not so sure anymore, what if all of this was a complete waste of time and I could have just spent it looking for her?' I turned away tears streaming down.

Reggie softly took my shoulders and turned me around

"You should have said something this is a huge burden to hold on your own" he held me then and I was so grateful and let out a flood of tears.

"Oh, I'm getting you all soaked," I said pulling back but feeling much better and smiling.

"Never mind that, come on let's go and have some fun".

We received our coats and hopped into the limo.

"Where to?" He grinned mischievously. "We still have the limo for a few hours."

He popped open a hatch on the side, which was a fridge with a bottle of bubbles and two glasses. "We can stay in here and do a loop of the city. It might be nice, and I do want to thank you."

I laughed and relaxed a little. "Sure, why not. And you don't have to thank me for anything."

"Oh, yes, I do. They all loved you this evening. My father and mother were impressed.

He stopped, poured the bubbles, and opened up the sunroof. He handed me a glass.

"Thank you, Angie. You didn't have to come but you did and it meant a lot, and your mother is out there somewhere, you have to keep believing that!'

We clinked glasses and popped out our heads into the New York evening. The wind went through my hair, and I let my thoughts drift away for once.

PURPLE FIRE

I was standing in the middle of our orchard back home. The full moon was high in the sky, flooding the whole area. I looked around, confused. How did I get back here? I smelled it before I saw it—smoke. I turned around and a fierce purple fire started of nowhere. It touched the first tree and melted like a candle in a split second, before spreading to the next and the next. I just stood there watching in horror until I was surrounded by a purple ring.

I woke up in a sweat, panting. It seemed so real! I jumped out of bed, ran into the corridor, and quickly called Dad.

He answered sleepily, "Angela? Are you okay? What time is it?"

"Dad?" I asked, urgently. "Is the orchard okay?"

"The orchard?"

"Yes, it's on fire!"

"You know our orchard alarm or house alarm would have been triggered, sweetheart. Even though I'm here in Florida, I would know. Are you okay?"

"Turn your video on Dad, so I can see you."

"You know I'm not good with that stuff. Hang on, let me try."

The phone muffled for a few seconds, and then I saw his tanned face.

"What is this all about, Angel?"

"Can you call the neighbors in the morning just to get them to check on everything, please?"

"Okay, I will. I promise".

I relaxed a little. "Okay, thank you".

"It's good to see you. What happened? What triggered this?"

"I just had a vivid dream, and I swore it was real. Sorry for waking you Dad, love you. I'll let you go back to sleep."

Dad yawned. "Okay, sweetheart. I will call you after I hear anything okay? Love you too."

Then he was gone.

I sat down on the corridor carpet. *It had seemed so real!*

The 5 AM alarm blared out, and I jumped up, grateful for the distraction.

I opened the door and Jayla was already out of bed. It was second nature to us now, and a normal part of the day.

"Did something happen?" she asked, indicating my phone.

"No, just a quick chat with Dad."

She had a big grin on her face. "How was last night? Any good gossip? I heard you came in quite early, was it awful?"

"It was fine, a lot of political smooching going on." I sat down next to her. "And I met James's girlfriend."

Jayla stood up. "Girlfriend? Seriously, what now?" she yelled.

I shushed her. "It's fine."

"Hell no, it's not fine. Where does he get off flirting with you, when he has a girlfriend?"

"They were together ages ago, and recently got back together."

Jayla started to get dressed vigorously.

"Wait 'till I see him, he's going to hear a thing or two …" Her voice was muffled as her top went over her head. "Seriously."

"Don't, Jay," I said. "Just leave it, okay?"

"This is not okay, Angie."

"I know, but I don't want a scene. If he wants to behave like that then let him, I'm going to be the bigger person."

Jay shook her head. "You're a better person than me, that's for sure. I'm still going to give him evil looks, you can't stop me from doing that."

I smiled. "Come on, let's go for our run."

Turns out, James wasn't our instructor for the run that morning, and he wasn't in tactics, either.

"He's sick," Jay said as we sat down for lunch. "More like chicken, if you ask me."

"Who's chicken?" Reggie asked, sitting down to join us.

Jay opened her mouth, but I kicked her under the table. "Ouch, what was that for?"

Reggie looked between them. "What's going on?"

Jay glared at me. "Ask Angie."

"It's nothing," I said, getting up from the table. "I will catch up with you later."

"Oh well, more lunch for me." Reggie grinned.

I stood outside the mess hall feeling slightly faint—not hungry. The thought of food made me nauseous. Reggie stepped out looking full and satisfied.

"Hey, what's up you're looking a little green".

"Yeah, I feel it, maybe I have been pushing myself a little too much lately"

I pulled him aside away from the entrance. "Reggie, can I ask you a favor?"

"Of course, anything".

"My mothers' files, as we haven't graduated yet we aren't allowed access to active cases, I can't get into my mothers, I'm sure there is nothing there and I was going to wait till after graduation but I need to see them. Do you have a way of accessing them?"

"Yes, I can help, let me make a call and I will meet you up there"

"Thanks, Reggie, means a lot"

I headed up to the library Josie, the head librarian, smiled at me when I came in. She looked like your classic stereotype: grey cardigan, glasses with the chain that hung around the ends of her glasses in case you lost them, and curled short grey hair. But I knew more lingered behind those alert eyes. I was dying to look into her and see, but even though a person can't tell I didn't want to pry into her feelings, and I liked Josie. Instead, I found out the old-fashioned way, we have become friends during the many hours I sat in here studying and researching my mothers' case. Josie would sit with me and she explained that she was an ex-police officer and a mighty good one at that. Three of her sons and her daughter had served. She lost a son and daughter during 9/11, and even though she was semi-retired, she couldn't bare to be too far from the Academy.

"Hi love, back again? You just let me know if you need anything, okay?"

"Thanks, Josie, will do."

I had decided that even though I didn't want to speak to Cayden I cannot ignore what his mother said about wanting to get to me I don't think leaving the base by myself was the best idea at the moment so had been spending more time here as of late.

I opened the police database on the computer. We weren't supposed to be accessing active cases. Technically the case was not active; it was only Dad and I that insisted it couldn't be closed, but no one was actively looking into my mothers' disappearance anymore.

I put my headphones on to some calming birdsong, while I was waiting for Reggie and read through some of the notes I had made so far. We were the last ones to see her before we went to bed so sometime in the night she would have left, I wrote down the portal on the page, was there a portal in my house? Is that how she left and why Police couldn't find any evidence? I pulled out the note she left. I stared at the I<3 NY sticker, I had a strong suspicion it was a huge clue, I underlined demon with a question mark, I stared at that and must have drifted off.

Christmas music filled the air. Mom, Dad, and I were sitting in the living room of our house with an open fire. I had a marshmallow on a stick toasting. Mom was laughing at one of Dad's terrible jokes, her face warm, glowing in the firelight. I pulled my marshmallow out, and it was covered in purple flames. I dropped it in fright and it fell to the carpet. A purple fire trail quickly raced across the lounge to the curtains, which immediately lit up. Then the Christmas tree started melting, the angel at the top the last ornament to be engulfed in flames. We all held each other and watched in horror. It was all happening so fast, there was nothing we could do.

"Angela, Angela, wake up!"

I sat up terrified. Josie the librarian was shaking me. I was trembling uncontrollably.

"Are you okay?" she asked, concerned. "You were crying out, it's late, dear, you should go for your supper before you miss it. I'm shutting up soon."

I looked at the time and jumped up. It was time for dinner, where was Reggie? He was supposed to meet me here. The thought of dinner made me feel nauseous. Something was wrong. I raced back to my dorm, which was empty, and sat on my bed. I turned my palm over to my birthmark and tried to ignite my flame ball. It started but quickly faded. I started to panic.

Oh no, now what? That dream felt so real; my heart was still racing. I reached for my journal, my hand shaking. As I grabbed it, my bag from the police ball fell on the floor. When I picked it up, a purple marble rolled out.

"What on earth is this?" I wondered out loud. Examining it closely, I saw it was a small glass ball with purple smoke inside.

"There you are!" Jay said, walking into the room. "How come you weren't at dinner? I was worried. It was your fave too, lasagna!"

I put the glass ball into my pocket. "I didn't feel like it. I wanted to do some research on Mom and catch up on my studies, was Reggie at dinner he was supposed to meet me at"

She sat down on the bed next to me. "He wasn't, weird for him to miss a meal. You never really talk about your mother, what happened?"

"That's why it's so hard to talk about," I said. Tears welled in my eyes as I looked away. "Nothing happened. She was with us on Christmas Eve. Everything was great … well, I thought it was. We were toasting marshmallows over the fire, and we had each given a present to each other. My mother collected angel Christmas ornaments, so Dad and I got her a special glass one to put on the top of the tree. She loved it so much, she cried when we gave it to her. I remember thinking at the time it was odd to see her cry, and she seemed more sad than happy with the gift. She had cooked my favorite for dinner."

"No way, lasagna?" Jay asked. "For Christmas?"

"It was Christmas Eve."

"Still," Jay said. "My family is all traveling, and usually just have snacks and red wine as we catch up. A lot of red wine."

I wiped my eyes. "Anyway, it was delicious, and not long after dinner we went to bed."

"Then what happened?" Jay asked.

"When I woke up in the morning, she was gone."

"That's it?" Jayla said. "Surely there must have been signs, evidence, did she leave a note?"

"At first, Dad and I thought she had gone for a walk to the neighbors. But then lunchtime rolled around, and we got worried, so we started calling around places she liked to go, the library, and antique furniture collectors, she loved to find special pieces. And the garden centers. She never really had any close friends—well, we didn't think so. It became evening and Dad called our local sheriff Sam. The next few days were a blur."

My eyes started to well up again, and Jayla grabbed my hand.

"Teams came in and scoured the house for evidence. Dogs came in to see if they could pick up trails. Everyone was interviewed, and posters were put up everywhere. But there was nothing, not even one lead. There was a sticker on the note my mother left, I pulled it out to show her, I think it means something and when I got into the Academy and being here, makes me feel like I'm one step closer to figuring it out but then someday it's a brick wall again.

"I'm so sorry Angie," Jayla said.

"The worst part is that, due to not finding any evidence at all, they think she just abandoned us or committed suicide, I'm not sure which is worse. But I know her, Jayla." I turned and looked at her. She also had tears in her eyes. "She wouldn't just leave us, and it sounds crazy, but I know she's alive. I can feel it!"

"If anyone can find her, you can," Jayla said. "Come on. Why don't you come out with Mike and me tonight? We are just going to watch a movie it will be an early one."

"No, I think I'll stay here if that's okay. I want to write in my journal."

"Okay I will stay with you, I don't think you should be alone Angie"

"I want to be, I need to rest and write for a bit".

"Ok but text me if you need anything, I'm going to jump in the shower and get ready."

I nodded, "Thanks, Jay."

I took the glass ball out of my pocket. Looking at it closely, I could see swirling purple smoke. It started to warm up. Smoke seeped out of the ball to swirl around me. I let go of it, but it floated in midair. Before I could react, I was transported through a smoke tunnel. It twisted me faster and faster in a spiraling corkscrew until suddenly it all stopped. I opened my eyes, my head spinning.

Two purple velvet chairs were facing an empty fireplace. I coughed the air was musty and dusty. I knew where I was, I was in the same underground tunnel I had followed Cayden to through that portal. Looking around, I there was rows and rows of books on the walls. On closer inspection, I didn't recognize any of the languages. The fireplace began to sizzle, and spark and purple smoke appeared. Kia flopped out in a burst and slithered towards a basket by the fire. More sizzling and sparking followed. Mrs. Montgomery appeared, and then Belinda.

I frantically tried to raise my fire. A small flame ball formed but fizzled out quickly. I started to panic and picked up a fireplace poker as a defense.

Belinda laughed. "What are you going to do with that, Angela? Poke our eyes out?"

"Hello, dear. Lovely to see you again," Mrs. Montgomery said.

"I wish I could say the same to you. How did I get here? Return me to the Academy at once!"

"Come now child, relax. Take a seat." She indicated to one of the velvet chairs as she sat down in the other. Kai slithered her giant head into her lap. "We intend you no harm … for now. We would like to chat. We have a proposition for you."

"I'll stand, thanks. And whatever it is, the answer is no."

"Oh, I'm sure you will want to hear what we have to say. Belinda didn't get a chance to finish the conversation at the ball. Now, wasn't that a lovely event? You looked stunning."

"You mean that puppet show? Because that's what everyone is to you, aren't they? Puppets to do with as you please and blackmail them—because otherwise, no one would be able to stand to be anywhere near you, including your son!"

Belinda stepped forward and a flame ball ignited. "How dare you talk to Mrs. M like that."

"Stand down Belinda, I will take care of this," Mrs. Montgomery said. "We don't make anyone do anything. Do you know how many humans want to be just like us, to have our powers? Those like Belinda here definitely have a choice and she has chosen power. Come now, don't pretend you're all innocent; you use your powers all of the time do you think those humans appreciate you nosing around in their minds without knowing." She stroked Kia's head, and her tongue swirled out in ecstasy.

"I'm nothing like you," I said, outraged.

"You're a demon, Angela. And whether you want to admit it or not, you like how the fire feels in your veins, how the surge of fire tingles your skin through your emotions. You enjoy power, and I think you will be very powerful … with the right training, of course."

"I don't need your help!"

"How is your fire, Angela?" Belinda sneered at me. "Seems like you had trouble igniting it when we arrived."

"I'm sure it will be back to normal soon; I'm just tired, that's all," I said.

"Have you been having any strange dreams lately?" Belinda asked.

"How do you know about those?"

"Don't they feel so real?" Belinda continued. "How did it make you feel to see your beloved family home and orchard be engulfed in flames? Purple flames are the hottest, you know. Things melt as soon as they're touched, and no ash or residue is left behind … it's like they never existed."

The hairs on my arms stood on their ends, and fear washed over me. "What have you done?" I whispered.

Mrs. Montgomery got out of her chair, to the annoyance of Kia, who was bored by all the talking and had gone to sleep.

"It's pretty complicated, and I won't go into the length and details, but in your simplified understanding, I have poisoned your fire."

"You did what?"

"Come now, my dear; you're not stupid. I'm sure you would have noticed how your fire is not responding to you, how tired you must feel, and the reoccurring nightmares. You have 'til the night before your graduation from that ghastly academy to decide to join us. If you don't, it will be too late to cure you—the poison will be too far gone, and even my glorious powers will not be able to bring you back. You belong with us, Angela. I know you like the power. Let us show you how to enhance it, how to train it, and together we will do amazing things."

"I will never join you!"

"Well, we'll see about that as you begin to weaken over the next few weeks. You have the glass ball—that is a direct portal to here. When you're ready to make the right choice, hold it up to your face for a few seconds, and it will transport you here. For now, you are dismissed."

She nodded at Belinda, who ignited a ball of purple smoke. Before I could respond she threw it at me, and I was once again thrust into a smoke vortex.

The 5 AM alarm blared and I sat up and groaned; my head was thumping.

Was it all a dream? I was still in my clothes from the night before; I reached into my pocket and pulled out the glass ball. Instead of just the smoke, it now had a clock that was counting down to graduation's eve.

What am I going to do? I flopped face-first into my pillow.

Jay popped up. "Come on sleepy, let's go before we get extra laps."

"This is a change," I said. "Look at you, all ready to go."

"Yeah, don't get used to it. My dad called super early. He was in his jet on a business trip and didn't realize the time."

"Everything okay?" I asked.

"Yep. He just reminded me I could still quit this, and that it wasn't too late to enroll in Harvard Law School."

"Sorry, Jay," I said.

Shaking it off, she said, "It's their way of showing they care. Okay, we got to move it."

As the day went on, my energy got more and more depleted. My run time was average, and at tactics, I got thoroughly beaten.

"Whitewing, a word," James said as tactics finished.

I walked over to him as the others hit the showers. "Yes," I said.

"What has gotten into you? You're better than this."

"Me?" I asked, still hurt. "This is the first time you've spoken to me since I met your girlfriend. I thought you were better than that too, James," I turned to walk away but I had to warn him. "You shouldn't trust her James, she is up to something, all my instincts say so."

"Angie, we can't do this here ok, let's find someplace and time to chat."

Feeling defeated I sighed and nodded as I turned back to the changing rooms.

I let the water and steam run over me. *What am I going to do? I don't want to die, would joining them be so bad?* I felt trapped, and I was running out of options. I could feel I was growing weaker by the day and didn't have the will to fight it anymore. I looked into my fire. It was weak, but it was there. *You want me to fight, don't you?* My hand was against the glass of the shower and it started to heat up. I took it off, and in its place was a heart drawn into the steam on the glass.

Okay. We need to make a plan.

I jumped out of the shower feeling a bit better. Jayla was waiting for me.

"What did His Majesty Instructor want?"

"He asked what was going on since I didn't do so well today."

"The nerve!" Jayla said, fuming.

"I know, but he has a point, Jay. I'm tired, I don't know if I can take another three weeks."

"You can't give up now, Angie. If anyone is meant to finish this, you are. You're the reason a lot of us keep going every day. You don't have to do this alone, you know."

I shrugged, knowing I couldn't tell her what I wanted to.

"Come on, it's free time for the rest of the day. How about just you and me go to the diner for a shake?"

"Sounds perfect." I smiled and hoped it was convincing. I didn't have the heart to tell her that was where James dumped me before we even got started.

We were almost out of the gate before Reggie shouted out, "Hey, where are you two off to?" He got closer to Mike, Jay linking her arms into his.

"Angie was feeling a bit over this place, so I thought a shake at the diner would be nice."

"Can we join?" Reggie asked.

Jay looked at me, unsure.

"Of course," I said, genuinely.

"Good, I'm starving!" Reggie exclaimed.

Reggie pulled me back as we were walking along to the diner.

"I'm so sorry I didn't meet you up at the library".

"Where were you? I asked.

"I made a call to one of my granddads' friends, I hope you don't mind but I told him about your mothers' case, don't worry he is extremely trustworthy. He told me I had to go and meet him so I used one of my free time slots.

"And what did he say?"

"He said he can't access the full Investigated file either, which was odd so he did some more digging and he said it's been referred to a paranormal agency.

My face drained of color but started to sweat at the same time.

"Angie are you ok?" Reggie asked concerned.

"Yes, I just need to sit down, Reggie please let's just keep this to ourselves ok."

"Of course."

We walked into the diner, and the jukebox was oddly silent. We all slid into the booth.

"What can I get y'all?" a waitress asked, as she came over with notebook and pen in hand.

"Why is the jukebox off?" I asked her.

"Oh, it got stuck on the same song, and everyone got tired of it. It'll get fixed next week."

"What song was it?" Jayla asked.

"'Don't Let Go by En Vogue," she said. "Ready to order?"

My mind was getting so foggy but it meant something for it to get stuck like that, was my mother trying to tell me not to give up?

"Yes, I'm starving!" Reggie said and started to rattle off his mammoth order.

"Earth to Angie. Angie?" Jayla asked.

"Huh?"

"You were far away. What do you want to eat?"

"Oh, just a chocolate shake and fries, please."

"That's it?" Reggie asked. "You need to build up those muscles so you can beat me. I have the best time right now. She'll have a double cheeseburger too, please," he told the waitress, who nodded.

"Whatever, Reggie, you won't keep that time for long,

and besides, is only five seconds faster than Angie's. Hardly counts!"

"Faster is still faster." He grinned.

My skin started to prickle and I could feel my birthmark heat up, I hadn't felt it for so long, and I almost cried in relief. I looked out the window to see if I could see Cayden.

The diner doorbell chimed as someone entered.

"Cayden? What are you doing here?" Reggie asked.

I wiped my head around, shocked to see him.

"I just wanted to have a word with Angela."

Jayla grinned, then whispered to me, "Where have you been hiding this dish, Angie?"

I slid out from the booth wordlessly, and Cayden indicated the booth by the door.

We both sat down, aware all eyes were on us.

"Cayden, are you crazy? Why did you come in? I thought you were trying to keep a low profile?"

"You didn't give me much choice. You aren't answering any of my demograms or coming to the range."

Before I could reply, he picked up my arm. My fire thickened.

"What's wrong with your fire?"

"I'm sick Cayden, and I'm scared," I said with tears in my eyes. Cayden looked at me with deep concern and pushed up the sleeve higher on my arm. His eyes widened with alarm.

"Angie, why are your flames purple?"

I whispered. "Lower your voice. I only have a few weeks to go before I graduate. I have been given a choice that comes with a time limit, I think it is a decision I must decide. "

He took my hand in his. "I'm not the enemy," he said, gently. "I want to help."

"I know that you do, Cayden, truly I do, but I need to do this on my own"

He released my hand.

I knew I was hurting him but I didn't want Cayden to go to war with his Mother, I didn't want to create a rift between them if I told him she had poisoned me I know there would be hell to pay. No matter what I couldn't get between them.

Cayden looked at me determined.

"Angie, I like you. I think our fires also like each other." He gave me a small smile. "I know you don't trust me, and in truth, I can't tell you everything. There is much you need to learn about demonic hierarchies. I am bonded to these rules with blood. It's not an excuse, but I want you to know I care deeply for you." He looked away. "It hurts to be apart from you for too long."

He looked into my eyes and held both my hands.

"Whatever is going on, we can face it together, be stronger together."

My heart was beating fast, and I could feel my fire willing me to accept his help.

A solitary tear rolled down my cheek. "Cayden, my fire wants you too, but it's not what my heart wants."

He let go of my hands. His face went from hurt to anger. "You want that human, don't you?" His face turned nasty. "You'll never be able to be fully intimate with him, without scorching him. No demon has that self-control." He stood up. "Besides, he seems to be very looked after right now with his Demon Slave. You can't compete with her."

"I don't think he loves her," I said, looking down.

"You think everything is about love. You have a lot to learn. Everyone wants power. The sooner you pop that bubble, the better." He stormed out of the diner.

In a second, Jayla slid in.

"What was all that about? Did he hurt you? Do you want me to hunt him down?"

"Just forget it," I said, wiping my eyes.

"Come on, let's eat. It will make you feel better."

"I'll be there in a sec." I gave her a half smile.

Jayla left me, unconvinced. I got up and went into the bathroom. Looking in the mirror, I could see the effects the purple fire was having on me. My skin was pale, the red streak in my hair dull. I could see the purple tinge under my skin.

I splashed water on my face and goosebumps ran down my spine. What scared me the most was my eyes, in the fluorescent lights, I could see a purple ring starting to surround my iris.

Struggling with every move, I went back to the booth keeping my eyes down when I could so as not to alarm anyone, and finished lunch with my friends. Jayla kept casting glances over to me every so often.

What am I going to do? I thought. Not even my fire responded, too weak.

That night I crawled into bed early. Jayla was off with Mike, happy to give me space. I looked at the pictures on the wall next to my bed. A new one of Reggie and I at the ball had been cut out and stuck up. His mother had sent me a copy of the New York Police monthly magazine, and we had been on one of the pages from the ball. His family was extremely proud, and Reggie's dad was calling him every week now to check in on his progress. Reggie had decided to come out to them after graduation.

Next to Reggie's photo was a picture of Mom, smiling she had the lights of the Christmas tree behind her, and her blonde hair was glowing like a halo. *What would you do,*

Mom? I closed my eyes, exhausted. My heart was beating slowly, and purple dots had started to appear on the inside of my eyelids.

I sat up in a cold sweat. I looked around my room. I could hear Jayla snoring. I jumped out of bed; there was a howling noise coming from the corridor.

I sneaked up and leaned against the door, which was vibrating. I opened it with a tiny crack. A purple flame smashed its way in. I backed up as fast as I could and watched in horror as the flames trailed up the sides of the wall, heading for Jayla's bed. I ran to her, but the flames were faster and circled her bed, cutting me off.

"No!" I screamed, tears streaming down my face as I fell to my knees. The flames rose high above me like a wave, then it came tumbling towards me. I closed my eyes.

I sat up again in a cold sweat, confused. I looked around. Jayla was softly snoring, but I didn't hear any howling. I jumped out of bed and opened the door to the hallway: nothing. I slid down the wall, relieved. Anger flooded through me. *This has to stop now! I can't be selfish I have to protect those that I love, it's not just about me, and isn't that why we all joined the Academy to start with? Faithful unto death.*

I took out the glass ball and as soon as I looked into it, I saw a cloud mixed with purple smoke then the tendrils came out to surround me. Again, I went tumbling through the vortex and opened my eyes. I was in the library.

Kia was curled up in her basket. She raised her head to hiss at me. Purple flames were crackling in the fireplace.

I stepped forward. The flames moved, and Belinda appeared.

"Ready to give in already?" she asked, smirking. "That last dream you had was a good one, wasn't it? I designed it myself."

I gritted my teeth. "I need to talk to Mrs. Montgomery."

"She doesn't just come when you demand it, you know. She's very powerful. You're lucky she even has an interest in you. Do you know how many mortals are begging to be who you are?"

I stepped forward to Kia, who again hissed at me.

The fireplace crackled, and Mrs. Montgomery appeared right beside Kia's basket. "What's this all about? Why have you upset Kia?" She looked up at me. "Back so soon, child?"

"I have a proposition for you."

"Do you?" She laughed. "I hardly think you are in a position to bargain."

"Do you want me to get rid of her?" Belinda asked, smiling.

"Stand down, let her talk," Mrs. Montgomery said, stroking Kia's head. Belinda crossed her arms, sulking.

"Graduating from the academy is important to me. I don't just want to finish; I want to be the best, and I can't do that with the purple fire poisoning my system. Let me graduate with my fire, and I won't only join you; I will do what I think you want."

"And what is that, child?"

"Marry Cayden."

Belinda uncrossed her arms and looked at Mrs. M.

"Well, aren't you the perceptive one," she said. "What made you think this would be so important that you could bargain with it?"

"I'm not stupid, and I do think he genuinely likes me, but it doesn't take a genius to see he is being puppeted from somewhere. All of this hardly seems a coincidence."

Mrs. M was silent for a minute. "I agree to your terms on one condition." She clicked her fingers, and a bracelet appeared in her hand.

"You have to wear this," she said.

"What is it?"

"It's a Demonic clasp. Don't worry, the humans won't be able to see that it's enchanted. It drips tiny amounts of the antidote into your bloodstream to keep the purple fire restricted. But it won't be completely gone. If you break our terms, it will also inject a more lethal amount, and you'll only have a few hours to live."

I bit my lip and felt cold all over. I knew I had no choice. I nodded.

"Good child. Belinda, attach this to her wrist." She passed the bracelet over to Belinda.

I held out my wrist. It was cold, not like metal but like liquid. It felt like ice water sitting on my skin. It molded to the shape of my wrist, and I felt a sharp pain. "Ow!"

"That's the first antidote being injected. It will be more the first time, as the purple fire is already deep into your bloodstream."

The effect was immediate. I could feel the warmth starting from my chest and moving through the rest of my body.

"Now, leave. Go and finish your precious training. But it's a waste of time if you ask me."

Before I could say anything, Belinda had already thrown a smoking ball at me, and the tendrils were surrounding me into a cage, and I was falling through the vortex.

THE PROPOSAL

I opened my eyes; the 5 AM alarm was blaring. I sat up, feeling my fire coursing through me. I looked at my arms and had never been so excited to see my fire squirming around.

I jumped out of bed and ran into the bathroom. My eyes were back! The purple was gone, and my skin was rosy.

Walking back to get changed for the run, I found Jayla groaning as usual. "I cannot wait 'til we graduate!"

"Come on," I said, pulling her out of bed. "You're going to want to see me get my best time back this morning!"

"Woah, what's gotten into you? You look refreshed. Don't tell me you snuck out to a spa without me."

"I wish," I said. "No, I just had a great sleep. Come on, let's go."

"All right, all right. Jeez," she said, grinning. "I think I kind of feel sorry for Reggie." She put her hand to her mouth. "Did I just say that? This place is making me soft."

I laughed. "Maybe, but I think I like this version of Jayla."

Still laughing, we stepped out into the morning air.

A layer of fog settled across the academy overnight, and with the sun not up, everything felt eerie.

"It feels like we're in a graveyard or something," Jayla said, shivering.

"Yeah, it's pretty spooky," I said, crossing my arms.

"Boo!" Reggie yelled, behind us. We both shrieked.

"Reggie!" Jay yelled. "What the hell!"

"Oh my god, that was amazing." He was breathless from laughing. "I got you girls so good."

"You're so going to pay for that," I said.

"Haha, it was just a bit of fun. Come on, I have the best time to keep."

"Yeah, well, let's just see about that."

We got to the race track and James was there. He nodded at me. And despite everything I felt like I have betrayed him and my heart for the commitment I made last night. I rubbed the demonic clasp even though no one else could see it, it sat coolly on my skin.

"Okay cadets, every test counts at this stage. With only a few weeks left to go, I have a bonus treats for the winner today. As you know, it's Thanksgiving this weekend. The Academy will be hosting a meal here for all the cadets. The lucky winner of today can invite someone to come to that dinner."

Now Jayla's head perked up. "For reals?" she asked.

"Yes, Miss Price."

"What about an extra helping of turkey too?" Reggie asked. Everyone laughed.

"Don't push your luck, Reggie. Okay, line up."

We all toed the line. I looked up; the sun was trying its hardest to push through the fog, an orange haze streaking through to us.

"On your marks. Get set. Go!" James started his timer and we all raced off.

We separated. With the fog, it felt like I was the only one running. My fire pumped along with my footsteps, the orange steaks encouraging me. It was a joy not to think, but to run with my fire, just us.

I crossed the finish line before I knew it, hardly even realizing it. Looking around, I was a bit confused.

"Congrats, Angie," James said as he handed me my water bottle. "A new best time, and I think also a new course record." He smiled. "It's good to have you back."

I smiled too.

Next came Reggie, and then Jayla puffed across the line.

Reggie crouched over, puffing. "What's in those shoes today, Angie? You have rockets or something attached?"

"Good on ya, girl," Jay said puffing and hugging me.

"Well done, Miss Price," James said. "That's the new best time for you. Nice to see you putting in some effort."

"Huff, just trying to beat Reggie," Jay said.

"Yeah, like that would have happened." Reggie grinned.

I smiled at my two friends.

"Anyway, I bet Angie is going to share her turkey with me!" Reggie said. "Who are you going to bring?"

"Um, I'm not sure, to be honest. I hadn't thought about it."

"You have a bit of time, you just need to let the office know their details for security before the dinner," James said.

The last of the cadets crossed the line.

"Okay, let's go extra drill today. Sit-ups, go!"

"For real?" Jayla mumbled.

We got down on the ground together and started to do our sit-ups.

"I don't have anyone to invite, Jay. My dad is away on a much-needed break, and I don't want to bother him."

"What about that delicious hunk that came into the diner?" Jay asked.

"Less chatter, more sit-ups, cadets!" James' voice boomed.

"Ouch," I said, and stopped to rub my wrist where the bracelet was.

"You, okay?" Jay asked.

"Yeah," I mumbled and continued my sit-ups.

James had us training most of the day and when we all got back to our dorms, we were exhausted. I needed to break to Cayden because I made the deal, at the end of the day I do care for Cayden and I don't want him to think I'm heartless.

As Jayla's snores filled the room, I jumped out of bed, heading towards the target grounds hoping he might be there. The fog was back with a vengeance, creating an eerie glow around the campus light poles.

I could feel him before I could see him, as usual, but this time I felt more than one presence. I held out my palm, and my flame appeared, not just to light my way but to have it ready in case Cayden was in trouble.

I got closer and Cayden was with someone but didn't look in trouble. They both turned as I arrived. I couldn't read Cayden; he had put on a tight poker face and didn't smile when he saw me. My fire, excited to be so near, started swirling around.

"Angela," Cayden said coolly. "Thank you for coming."

"Sure. I just wanted to talk to you, but I wasn't sure if you would be here."

"Because it's been hard to find time with you I put an enchantment close to this area, so if you do cross over, I know you're here." He said as a matter of fact.

"Right," I said. "Who's this?"

A tall man stood next to Cayden with a hooded cloak. His features were fine and his skin was almost translucent. He had bright red eyes that looked at me, unimpressed.

"Angela Whitewing, meet Jerico."

Jerico nodded. "It is a pleasure to meet you, Angela."

His words were very precise, like each letter had been thought out, or said a million times.

I swallowed, suddenly nervous. "Hi, Jerico."

"Jerico has come because my mother has just informed me that we are to be married." He looked at me then, his guard slightly down now like he was disappointed.

"I … I … well, yes," I stammered. I didn't know what to say. Cayden can we please talk just the two of us, I would like to explain.

"I am here, Miss Whitewing, on behalf of the Montgomery Lineage. You see, Cayden is of Royal blood, and because of this, certain formalities and traditions must be carried out." Jerico said interrupting me.

"I understand that but I would like a minute with Cayden please".

Jerico looked at Cayden who nodded his head.

"Will you please excuse us, Jerico?" Cayden said. "I need to talk to Angela in private."

"Of course, sire." Jerico walked away towards the trees.

Cayden rushed toward me. "What have you done? Do you have any idea what you've started?"

We sat down on the bench. 'You said you wanted to help' I said trying to make light of the situation.

"Come on Angie, you know this is not what I meant".

"Would the thought of marrying me be that bad?" I said genuinely

He took my hand. "Angie, I care for you deeply, you know that, is this truly what you want?'

He looked into my eyes, and all his protective shields melted away.

I gasped it was the first time he had done that, he put his whole soul bare for me to see. I saw his anguish for Rebecca, his hopelessness for not being able to help me, and his defeat for his mother but most of all I saw his love for me.

Our lips found each other. It was fierce at first, our fires dancing and swirling. I had never felt anything like it; my palm burned, and I could feel his palm burning on the back of my neck, my thoughts drifted to James feeling conflicted for a second before Cayden pulled me onto his lap and our body heat intensified, it was impossible to tell whose fire was whose as our kissing increased. Cayden reached up and tenderly put his hands to my face and slowly reluctantly pulled us apart.

"Jerico will be back soon Angie we should stop". I nodded, and he held me to his chest. For a moment I closed my eyes, badly wanting to believe that this was where I belonged. I moved from his embrace. He held my hands.

"Cayden, I owe you an explanation," I said.

"Yes, you do, but unfortunately now is not the time. Jerico will be back in a few minutes, and he has to report to the family. Just listen to what he has to say and it will be over … well, this part, at least."

"I did come here also to invite you to something," I said, tumbling it out.

"You did? What is it?"

"I'm allowed to invite someone to our Thanksgiving feast the Academy is putting on this weekend and wondered if you wanted to come?"

A mixture of emotions fluttered across his face and I thought for a moment he was going to say no.

"Yes, of course, I'll come. It will be nice to be a part of your human life that is so important to you." He smiled.

Jerico walked towards us.

I numbly stood there as Jerico outlined all of the staged protocols required. He explained that the Montgomery clan is one of the oldest of the five royal demonic families since time began and with that comes many older traditions which included wearing a blood-red dress and of course, no humans were allowed at the wedding It felt like I was underwater—everything was muffled. My fire seemed happy and like this is all normal but my own internal emotions were completely conflicted.

We shared an awkward goodbye once he was finished. I walked back to my dorm like a zombie.

I lay awake on my bed fully clothed. Images of blood-red, lacy wedding dresses flickered around in my head. I had never imagined my wedding, but a blood-red dress, now that I thought of it, was not something I would have picked. Along with that, no humans were allowed, so my dad couldn't come. Maybe that was a good thing, I had no idea how I was going to tell him about any of this, or even if I should. Maybe I could bring Jay and Reggie, they know a bit about what's going on, and I bet they would understand and keep the secret. *Angela Montgomery. I guess it has a nice ring to it. But then, why do I feel so sick?* My fire seemed very happy about the whole thing. I stared at the bracelet on my wrist, keeping the purple fire away. *It won't be so bad. Lots of couples are in arranged marriages, right?* I groaned and rolled over, willing to sleep.

THE TEST

"Whitewing, are you listening?" Reggie asked.

"Huh?" I asked.

"Wow, you're distracted today. What's up?"

We were sitting in the library going over our assigned cases. Everyone had a cold case; The Academy was always hopeful for new clues that may open the cases back up. After we graduated, we all were assigned our time as beat cops but after that many wouldn't want to be a detective, like Jay she wanted to as she puts it 'fight bad guys on the streets" I smiled to myself she made me laugh so much. We had to report our findings as our last assessment before we graduated. I asked for special circumstances to do mine for my mother. It was declined due to personal circumstances, but it was agreed that I could do it as an extra assignment on top of what was assigned to me.

"Oh nothing," I said. "I was just thinking about the Thanksgiving feast."

"Have you decided whom you're taking?"

"Yes, I have." I managed a half smile.

Sarcastically, Reggie said, "And you look excited about it."

"No, I am. I'm just tired, that's all. We have a lot going on."

"Yeah, tell me about it." He looked down at the picture of my mother that was in my case file. "She was really beautiful."

"Is," I corrected him. "She is beautiful.

"Well, if anyone can crack the case, Angie, I'm sure it's you!"

"Thanks, Reggie," I said, the smile not reaching my eyes.

"When we graduate can I visit your grandfathers' friend, I would like to know if we can figure out some connections to the Paranormal Agency, I want to talk to someone there.

"Not sure if he can even help Angie as he seemed to think it's all very hush-hush and he hadn't even seen a case file with that assignment before. But of course, it's a good start."

Just then Jayla bounded in. "Guess what, guys!" she boomed.

Josie the librarian shushed her.

I laughed. "Hi Jay, what's going on?"

"You'll never guess what," she said in a loud whisper. "Mike has asked me to come home with him after graduation to meet his family for Christmas!"

"Oh, I'm so excited for you Jay." We hugged.

"Most important question," Reggie said. "What are you going to wear?"

Jay's face dropped. "Reggie, I hadn't thought of that. You have to help me!"

Reggie was starting to get quite the reputation as a fashion consultant; after the ball, everyone had heard about Reggie's sense of style. More of the cadets—both men and women—were asking for his help. He was delighted and I was so happy for him.

As they both went into all the choices of shoes Jay should consider, my mind drifted off again.

A demogram had arrived first thing this morning after our run when Jay was in the shower. It was from Jerico, wanting my opinion on the wedding dinner. I wasn't even sure why he was asking—to be polite, I thought. Half of it grossed me out, there were lots of different types of animal entrails, and the other half … I didn't even know what it was.

Another demogram arrived almost straight after from Cayden, swearing most of the food was purely for ceremonial purposes, from long traditions to show respect to the underworld and after we'd go and get a shake and burger. I had to smile at that; I don't think I could have pretended to enjoy goats' brains and fried snakes.

"Yes, no socks. You have perfect feet, and a splash of red on your toenails and it would be perfect!" Reggie said.

"What do you think, Angie?" Jayla asked.

"Huh?" I asked, again.

"My feet! Do you think they're cute?" Jayla had taken her shoes and socks off and was wiggling them at me.

"Why on earth do you want to know if your feet are cute?"

"Haven't you been listening? We're debating whether to wear socks inside or go barefoot after I take my boots off. Reggie says no socks. I'm not so sure."

I laughed and shook my head. "I love that this is your biggest concern right now. I agree with Reggie—your feet are cute, no socks for sure."

Reggie looked triumphant. "See!" he said.

"Fine, but if I get kicked out, it's your fault."

"You won't, they will love you," I said.

Jayla beamed. "What are you going to wear for tomorrow?"

"What do you mean?"

"For Thanksgiving."

"What about it?" I asked, still not getting what Jay was saying.

"We can wear whatever we want tomorrow, we don't have to wear a uniform," Reggie said. "Where have you been? My room has been a train station with everyone wanting some styling tips."

"What's the big deal, anyway?" I asked.

"Unlike you, not all of us have gotten to dress up for the longest time, and get out of this dusty uniform."

"You're right, I'm sorry. To be honest, I hadn't thought about it."

"Okay, let's go sort it right now!" Jay insisted.

"I want to spend some time on my assignment," I replied.

Jay grabbed my hands, pulling me up. "Oh, come on Angie, you want to look good for your guest."

I felt so much warmth towards these two but guilty too, they didn't even know I had got engaged, maybe we could both pull them aside tomorrow to tell them.

"She has a point," Reggie said.

"Okay, okay," I said, grinning at them. "Let's go."

The rest of the afternoon—whether I liked it or not—was all fashion. It wasn't something I cared for, but they did and it made them happy. So, I gladly acted as their puppet as they pulled me in and out of various outfit choices.

THANKSGIVING

Thanksgiving was here, and I couldn't sit still. I was nervous; we were given the day as leave but confined to the Academy.

Important faculty and visitors were coming in but overall, the mood was happy, and the buzz of graduating and seeing family and friends soon was getting closer.

A demogram had popped in as soon as Jay was out. *'Can't wait to see you'* was all it said before it fizzled away. To my surprise, I was looking forward to seeing him too. It was a nice feeling, to have something to look forward to and someone to share it with.

I wiped my hands on my skirt which felt so soft under my hands. The final outfit choice decided by the committee was an A-line red velvet pleated skirt with a long-sleeved black lace top tucked into it. It highlighted the red streak in my hair which thanks to the antidote were back to its full luster, and had been curled expertly by Jay; it tumbled down my back. I loved the feel of the velvet, another Reggie special. He was good at this!

Jay was right: it felt great to get out of uniform for a bit.

I threw on my big coat and boots; it was cold outside now, winter fully on our doorstep. I needed to pick up Cayden at the Academy gates. My fire kept me pretty warm most of the time, but I knew that if I didn't wear a coat, I would get some questionable looks.

Cayden was waiting outside the security booth. His face lit up when he saw me, and my fire jumped in delight. Once we were all signed in and a shiny visitors badge was on his top, he turned to me.

"You look stunning, Angie."

"You're not too bad yourself." I smiled. He had on some black shiny shoes, a crisp white collared shirt, black trousers, and—ironically—a deep red jacket.

"Everyone will think we collaborated on our outfits."

"Well, I guess we are more in sync than we thought we were."

He smiled and offered me his arm and I took it as we walked towards the mess hall.

Stepping inside, I removed my coat and couldn't believe what I was seeing. The hall had been completely transformed; lights grew along the walls like vines and then hung down from the ceiling with rows of leaves. Tables were set up, and each one was beautifully decorated with flowers, leaves, and all colors of the season.

Jay came up to us. "Isn't it incredible!"

"Who did this?" I asked.

"Mike told me it was the instructors," Jay said.

James then came up to us. "It's our way of giving back, acknowledging the hard work you have all put in. We are thankful for all of you." He looked at Cayden. "You must be Angie's guest. I saw you at the ball too. I haven't formally introduced myself." He held out his hand. "Hi, I'm James, the head instructor here."

"Nice to properly meet you, James. I'm Cayden, Angela's fiancé."

James dropped Cayden's hand as if burned. My heart started beating frantically, and I sucked in my breath. *Did he just say what I think he said?*

Jay jumped on me. "For real! Omg, girl!" She hugged me so tight; it was suffocating. I just let her, frozen in shock.

"Congratulations, Angela," a snaky voice said from behind me. "It will be an absolute pleasure to have you in the family." It was Mrs. Montgomery. And standing next to her looking triumphant was her Demon Slave Belinda.

Jay let go of me.

"Thank you," was all I could manage, I couldn't believe she was here, what was she doing here, I looked to Cayden hoping he hadn't kept this from me.

"Mother," Cayden said. "I didn't know you would be here."

"Well, as a beneficiary to the Academy, I was invited, and thought I would come there is a lot to be thankful for." and she stared right at me.

Kia, sitting around her neck as a scarf, chose that moment to hiss at me. I wanted to poke my tongue out at her but knew that would look strange. Cayden squeezed my hand in support, he could also see Kia.

"Cayden, come over and see where we're sitting," I said as I pulled him away from everyone's judging looks.

Jay, thankfully getting the cue, offered to show Mrs. Montgomery around the mess hall to see some of the memorabilia.

"Did you know your mother was going to be here?" I whispered loudly to Cayden.

"No, I swear Angie I didn't that's why I asked?"

He looked genuine so I decided to let it go.

"Ok but why did you tell James about our engagement, we haven't discussed when we were going to tell people".

"He's always lurking around you, it kind of slipped out."

"That's not your decision to make!"

"Isn't it? We're both getting married, Angie. This isn't just about you."

I let out a breath and some of the fights went out of me. "Yes, of course, but we could have discussed when a good time would have been to tell everyone. I haven't even told my dad yet."

Cayden grabbed my hand. "You're right, I'm sorry. I'm just excited. But I'll tone it down and let you lead the way with the announcements from now on. Speaking of which, we have to lock in the date—Jerico is bugging me constantly."

I nodded. "For now, let's sit and enjoy today, and this feast." I forced a smile. This was all going way too fast for my liking; my feelings for Cayden were strong, but I didn't fully trust him, and I wasn't ready to marry him. I was running out of options pretty quickly.

We sat near the head of the table, Cayden on the side of me that was closest to his mother, who was at the head of the table. James was next to her and of course so was James's girlfriend, Belinda. She winked at me, seeming quite smug. James was avoiding my eye contact completely.

"Is it true?" Reggie asked. He was sitting next to me on the other side. "Why didn't you tell us?" He looked concerned. "Is this what you want?"

"It just happened. I'm sorry I didn't tell you I didn't mean to not tell you. It was all so quick I'm still digesting it."

"You didn't answer my question. Is this what you want?"

I put my hand over his, and whispered, "It's complicated, Reggie. Please just leave it for now. Cayden is a good man can we please just enjoy this dinner?"

"Okay Angie, I'll let it go. For now."

The dinner was delicious, and all of the speeches were wonderful. I truly did feel grateful for so many things.

I loved watching my friends get to know Cayden, they are so incredible to accept him and make an effort, and it looked like Cayden and Mike—who was sitting opposite him—seemed to hit it off.

And, despite everything, I enjoyed myself. Most of the people I loved in the world were in one place. I wished my wedding reception could be like this. Maybe Jerico would be open to a human version after the official one. I couldn't believe I was already starting to think about it all seriously.

Cayden said his goodbyes to everyone except James, who chose not to be around. I walked him back to the security gates.

"Thanks for inviting me. I had a really good time. Your friends are amazing and very protective of you," he said.

"I know. I'm very grateful for them."

He leaned in and kissed me on my cheek. I smiled.

"I'll be in touch. We should discuss our plans and where you'll be living after next week."

I nodded, feeling a bit faint. I had wanted to move in with Jay after graduation both of us had started to look for where we wanted to go next. We wanted to stay in New York, and Jay's parents owned a small apartment they used for traveling in and out of the city. I, of course, wanted to pay my share once I was set up. Now that we were getting married, I bet Cayden's Mother would not hear of me living with a human.

He walked through the security gates. I waved and turned. I sighed, feeling a weight lift.

I hadn't walked far when James appeared. I kept on walking.

"Wait, Angie. Please, let me clear the air."

I sat down at a nearby bench. Some snow flurries were coming down and even though it wasn't that late, it was almost dark. A lamppost illuminated us.

"You can't marry him, Angie. He isn't right for you," James said.

Anger swelled up inside me. "And how would you know, James? You don't know me. Cayden is a good man. He's been there for me when …" I trailed off.

"When I wasn't," he finished.

"It's not like you're a good judge of character. Belinda is a monster. You can't even see what's right in front of you," I snarled. I knew this was unfair, as humans couldn't see the spell, but I didn't care.

"I don't think she's a monster, but I agree—something is not quite adding up. So I just broke up with her."

"You did what?" I said, the anger falling away.

"I know it sounds cliché, but seeing you with Cayden and hearing your news made me realize exactly what I do and don't want." He held my gloved hand in his. "Angie, I know I started then stopped, and put up too many rules and walls, but I truly thought I was protecting you and your career. I can see I should have gone about it another way."

"James, you knew how I felt about you, and you strung me along only to dump me, but then you already had a girlfriend. Even if I did want this, it's too late now," I said, tears starting to well.

"It's not, Angie. You graduate in a week and then you won't be a cadet anymore. We can be together, fight crime together." He smiled and wiped away a tear that had escaped.

The flurries had turned into snow, falling harder.

Despite myself, I smiled. "That does sound fun." I stood up. "I can't, James. This isn't just about you and me, I wish I could explain, but I need to be responsible for the path I have been given. One day I hope I can explain it to you." I wiped away another tear.

James stood up too. "Angie…"

"I'm sorry James." I turned and half walked, half ran away from him. The moment I turned away the tears cascaded down my cheeks like a waterfall.

I made it to my room without anyone seeing me. Grateful it was empty, I sobbed into my pillow. How could I ever be with James without burning him alive? I could never do that to him, or any other human. I cried and cried as I succumbed to my fate. This was the life that I must lead—my path was decided. I felt my fire try to console me, wrapping a warm glow around my body like a cocoon.

I must have fallen asleep like that because when I next opened my eyes it was dark and a blanket was over me. Jay must have placed it there before she went to sleep. I could hear her quiet snores come from her bed.

A green glow attracted my attention—a demogram from Cayden. But right beside it was a purple one.

I opened up the green one. *Thank you for sharing an important part of your life with me, I can't wait to show you what will be ours. Cx*

A pang of guilt hit me as the message puffed away. I opened up the purple one.

One week to go. Don't mess this up. Mrs. M.

QUESTIONS

For the next few days, I was glad for once that the Academy had us so busy mentally and physically. Reggie hadn't brought up the engagement again, although I could tell he was bursting with questions. We were all tired this week, what with finals and everything. There were the final presentations of our findings for our cases, the last physical challenges, and we had heard rumors of a challenge mission. This rumor had passed down from cadets' classes through the years. It was different every year, but it could make or break your finishing. We were all feeling a bit jumpy.

"You still here, dear?"

Josie interrupted my thoughts.

"Yes, just cramming in a few more test exams," I said.

She indicated my notes on my mother. "Did you find anything new?"

I sighed. "No, as far as I can tell, there isn't much to go on. I was going to talk to my dad after graduation to close the case officially. I don't think I can truly help others if I keep looking for evidence on my mother that maybe isn't there to start with."

"What do you mean?"

"I still believe in my heart she would never have left us unless it was life or death" I blinked and rubbed at the tears that always threatened to fall when I talked about my mother. "I feel like I'm going around in circles and finding out half-truths."

"Oh, honey." Josie sat down and put her arm around me.

"That is part of it, your job is to figure out what is true and what isn't, sometimes we are looking so hard to find something we don't even see what's in front of us".

I wiped away the tears and shut my mother's case firmly.

"It's time. I have a future of my own that needs me; I have friends ... and a fiancé. It's time I take responsibility for my own life. Thank you for all of your support and for taking the time to stop and listen. I hope that I can repay you the favor one day."

"You will, I have no doubt," she said, and gave me a huge hug; the smell of apple tree blossoms hung in the air.

"Do one thing for me before you leave, okay?" she asked.

"Anything," I said.

"Follow your mark; it holds the truth that you seek." She smiled and walked away back to her trolley of books to shelve.

"Was she talking about my Demon Mark? No way, not possible I said to myself, as I packed up my books.

Reggie was waiting outside for me. It was dark; there was no snow, but the air was icy.

"Reggie, what're you doing here?"

"You didn't think I would let you get away that easily?" he asked.

I laughed. "No, of course not. But you aren't going to make me change my mind."

He locked arms with mine. "You're so young, why get married so soon? You have a great sea of fish to swim in and try first."

"Fish? Reggie?"

"Okay, maybe not fish, but you know what I mean. Angie, you haven't lived; you need to have some fun."

"Love is love, though, isn't it?" I asked.

"But you don't love him, I can see it in your face. Yes, he is special to you, no doubt, but you aren't in love with him."

"That can come," I said. "He is special, and we do share a strong bond." I desperately wanted to confide in Reggie about my fire, about everything, but I knew how dangerous that would be for him.

Reggie sighed. "Well, I hope at least I can be a groomsmaid?"

I laughed. "Oh Reggie, I can't promise that. His family has many … traditions. But I'll be confiding in you for all things wedding dresses."

"I guess that's acceptable."

We walked in comfortable silence for a bit until we reached my dorm.

"Thanks for the walk." I hugged him.

"You know where I live." He smiled.

I woke up startled, my fire thumping like crazy. It was the middle of the night, and someone was in my room.

"Whitewing, wake up!" James whispered urgently next to my bed.

"James, what's going on?"

"Be as quiet as you can. Get dressed, don't forget your coat, and meet me in the corridor."

I jumped as quietly as I could out of bed and dressed quickly, grabbing my coat.

Out in the corridor, all of the instructors were there.

"Whitewing, we're kidnapping you," James said.

My fire pumped. "You're what?"

"We usually wouldn't brief the cadet in person 'til after the deed and the assessment is complete," one of the other instructors piped up.

"Because you have been through this already, Angela," James continued, "We didn't want to frighten you."

"I can handle it," I said, sticking out my chin.

"Angela Whitewing," James said, all official now. "We have chosen you because many cadets have a close bond with you. We want to test them emotionally, physically, and mentally. Yours and their performance during this exercise will determine your outcome at graduation, and ready you for the real world, do you accept?"

"I do," I said, defiantly.

"You will be bound and blindfolded then taken to a secure location to await rescue."

Before I could reply, James bound my arms behind my back and applied a blindfold to me. He guided me downstairs. It took all of my self-control to not burn through the bindings; my fire was under colossal protest.

I heard a van door open, and was pulled in and seated; around me, the Academy emergency siren went off.

The final test had begun.

FINAL TEST

The van ride was bumpy and went on for a while; I counted thirty minutes so far. I had tried to make a map of where we were going in my head like we were trained to do. I tried to hone my senses too and listen for any telling sounds but all I could hear were the noises coming from the van and my fire swirling close to my ear drums angry that we were not attempting to escape.

After about fifteen more minutes, the van stopped. There were some murmurings outside, and then they moved me into what I thought was another van—they made a decoy.

The door slid shut, and after around twenty minutes, the road got windier. I could hear tree branches scrape along the roof of the van and scratch past the windows. Ten more minutes and the van stopped; we were roughly seventy-five minutes away from the Academy.

The van door opened, and I was carried out gently onto the pavement, then stairs—wooden, by the sound of our shoes. When the blindfold was removed, I blinked, adjusting to the light; I was in a wooden cabin of some kind. It smelled homey, not like a kidnapping location. A fire occasionally crackled in the corner. I looked around, and James stood there.

"James?" I said. "Where are we?"

"Welcome to my family cabin. We used to come here a lot as kids—not so much anymore, but I try to get out here at least once a year if I can."

"Feels too cozy to be a kidnapping hideout and why the blindfold it's not like I can tell anyone."

He smiled. "Well, we don't want you to freeze, blindfold for practice for you, this could happen in the future and this is a test of your reactions and coping mechanisms too."

"How does it work? How do the others know where to go?"

"We placed all sorts of clues, and one of the other instructors will pretend to be the criminal and call into the team leaders with their list of demands."

"Who are the leaders?"

"Reggie and Jayla. Why?"

I smiled. "That's great; they both deserve some time to shine. Can I get out of these?" I asked, indicating the handcuffs.

"No, we have to try to at least be a bit authentic, but I can loosen them a bit for you."

James bent down close to me; I could smell his aftershave and his minty hair shampoo.

"Ouch," I yelped.

"Sorry, did I hurt you?"

"It's okay; the chain just pinched my skin".

But it wasn't okay, my mark was burning on my palm, and my fire had started to pump.

A second later, the door opened, and Belinda walked in.

"Belinda?" James asked. "What are you doing here? Is this about us? Now is not the time; we're in the middle of the cadets' final practical assessment."

"James" I yelled jumping up from the chair, "release me quick from the handcuffs"

"It's not you that I'm here for, James." She turned her attention to me. "I'm here for Angel." She smirked.

"What? I don't understand."

"James," I said. "Listen to me, you have to go, now. Run, James!"

"Oh, this is so boring," Belinda said and shot a ball of smoking gas at James. He froze on the spot, his eyes stuck in a state of confusion.

"James!" I screamed. "What did you do to him?"

"I petrified him; he'll slowly turn to stone. Don't you think he will make a handsome statue?"

The door opened again, and a man walked in; I felt my fire retreat, suddenly afraid.

"Hello, Miss New York Police Cadet. We meet again," he said, looking delighted.

I swallowed a lump in my throat, it was the other Demon Slave from the sewers and I swore I could smell burning flesh; I sat back down on the chair.

"What, not even going to try and escape?" he sneered.

"I'm not leaving James," I spoke up, sounding braver than I felt. "Why are you here?" I knew I had to keep them stalled as long as possible, hoping that Cayden would get to us.

"Revenge, of course, sweetie." He leaned down to me "As much as I loved the redecorating you did to my hands …" He took off the gloves he was wearing; they still looked raw, pink but healing, and some of the skin was yellow and peeling. "I just wanted to thank you in person. And we didn't get to finish our chat."

"Wait 'til Mrs. Montgomery hears about this," I said.

Belinda stepped forward. "Oh, we don't care about her. I'm more powerful than her and the stupid snake now; I got what I needed. She was just a pawn in our plan."

I looked between them. "It was obvious you didn't want to be with James, but why the big charade?"

"Him?" Belinda laughed. "Don't insult me; he's a mere mortal. I was just with him to be closer to you. It's Treston that I love." They started to make out, and I quickly leaned over James; he was still breathing, thank goodness.

"Right, enough chit-chat, let's get this show on the road," Treston said.

"But what are you going to do with me?" I asked, doing my best to keep them talking as long as possible.

Treston nodded to Belinda, "It's your marvelous plan, babe; you tell her."

She trailed a fingernail up the inside of my arm; my fire squirmed under her touch.

"We all sense great power in you. As untrained as you are, all of that glorious fire is going to waste. I want it. I knew Mrs. M's strength was her purple fire; now that I have that under my control, I manipulated both of you to weaken your defenses. What you have will be mine!"

"And what exactly are you going to do with all of this so-called power?"

Belinda laughed "Oh that's right Cayden never actually told you did he about the Royal Demon families".

"He did actually, well he told me they existed and that to be a Montgomery there were certain protocols."

"What he didn't tell you is that each family has a specific fire, the matriarch of this family holds the flame the hottest, it is only the royal families that can wield the different flames of power, Montgomery holds Purple. If you control all the royal flames, you cannot be defeated.

That is why Mrs. M wanted you, your fire is not from any royal lineage that they can find, they are still searching through ancient texts but you are an anomaly. By combining yours with theirs by producing a new offspring the Montgomery lines' power would increase trifold.

"Wait, what, offspring?!"

"Come on Angela, I didn't take you for stupid, why do you think Cayden was sent to be so close to you, this was a setup from the very beginning even as far as Rebecca".

"What about Rebecca?"

"She wanted to be a Demon Slave, it wasn't all Cayden's fault, some humans are not as robust as others, and more often than not our internal organs cannot handle the change and the combination with the demonic fire. So, she internally combusted'. But it was the perfect opportunity to get Cayden close to you".

"That's horrible, poor Rebecca, does Cayden know?"

"Rebecca knew the risks and no Cayden does not know, but what does it matter now, you won't be around much longer to tell him."

She leaned down to my handcuffed wrist and before I could catch on to what she was up to, a hot flame shot out of her finger, snaked around the bracelet, and shattered it. Hot liquid filled my veins. I screamed as it forced its way through my fire, my limbs, and my senses; receiving that much purple fire poison at once was like swallowing acid.

I fell to the ground; it was everywhere. I could taste it, smell it, and I knew when I opened my eyes, I would see everything in a purple haze.

"Get her up," Treston said. "Let's get underground. Take the stone lump with us."

Belinda cast her purple smoke around us, and soon we were falling through a vortex. I landed hard; it was cold and damp and smelled like sewers. James landed next to me.

I used all my strength to sit up, my hands still cuffed. My head was spinning, and everything had a purple tinge. I scrambled over to James; he was colder now, his pulse slower. We didn't have much time. How were the cadets going to find us here?

Belinda picked me up, threw me onto a wooden table—smashing the handcuffs—and locked my legs and arms down.

"She doesn't have much time left; make it quick, get the others," Belinda said to Treston.

I looked around; I was in some sort of ceremonial room, lit by lanterns and candles creating a warm glow. In the corner sat all sorts of what looked like medieval torture equipment.

"This won't work," I said to Belinda, "you don't even know what to do. That equipment looks older than time itself."

My head reeled to the side in shock as she slapped me.

"Oh, I have been waiting to do that for so long, ever since the police ball. You think you're so unique, so smug. You have no idea what you're stepping into. You don't deserve all of the privileges that they gave to you on a silver platter; you didn't even take it! Do you know what we would give up for that kind of power, to marry into a Royal family and have your powers without going through an agonizing transformation? You're so weak. I'm going to suck out your fire and combine it with ours and share it with my kind, and we're going to make a new royal line that's more powerful than anything before."

I spat blood at her from the cut on my lip.

"You're going to pay for that."

"Enough!" Treston roared. Behind him were five more shapes, creatures all in different states of shifting in and out of human form. They surrounded me and held hands.

I squirmed; the poison was getting worse and my legs were starting to go numb.

Belinda started to chant in a language I hadn't heard before, but somehow, I was able to understand what she was saying. The others started to join in, tendrils of red fire began to come out of my body, and they started to make a ring around the chanting circle.

"No!" I shouted. "No, no, it's my fire, you can't take it." I started to cry, but it was useless. No one knew we were here.

The poison was spreading faster now that my fire was flowing out. I couldn't move my legs, and it was rapidly coming down my arms and torso. I felt faint and dizzy. *Is this it?* I shut my eyes, determined to hold onto memories of my friends and family. I smiled as tears ran down my face. I had joined the Police Academy because I wanted to find my mother, but what I found was just as important: love and friendship. Despite everything, I was happy to be me.

"I'm with you," a voice whispered, so far away.

"Mother?"

"You have always known deep inside who you are," the voice whispered.

My mark started to glow, brighter and brighter.

"Look, Angel, the signs have been with you always." The voice faded.

"Mother, don't leave me. I need you," I pleaded.

"Follow the message I left you it will guide you to me when the time is right. I love you so much." And she was gone.

Images flashed into my vision: the A4A carving in my father's desk that my mother made; the nurse in the hospital; Josie; my actual image in the mirror.

Kia apparated into the room behind the circle, followed

by Mrs. Montgomery and Cayden—even with only a fraction of my fire left, I still felt him.

I opened my eyes. The smell of apple tree blossoms passed by my nostrils. My mark grew hot as tendrils of white light reached out like fingers and caressed the strings of fire leaving my body, then formed into the shape of giant angel wings that spread like a blanket over me. I clicked my fingers and there was a massive explosion. All of the demon slaves flew from the circle into the air where they hung, suspended.

I sat up, all the bonds shattering free. Cayden moved toward me but his mother held him back. I rushed to James, placing my palm above his heart; It felt like warm butter moving under my skin as I spread the glow through the cold stone until it smashed. He was cold, too cold.

"James," I whispered. A tear fell down my cheek. "Come back to me."

I held him in my arms, my hand on his heart. Slowly I could hear his heart start to beat and pump blood into his limbs. He sucked in a breath.

"Welcome back." I smiled at him, then kissed him with all of me; it felt so good. And he kissed me right back.

"I had the strangest dream," he said. "I hope I'm not still dreaming."

Mrs. M cleared her throat. Cayden rushed to my side. I stood and helped James up.

"We came as soon as my mother got an alert that you were getting poisoned," Cayden said.

"Did she tell you that she was the one that had me poisoned to start with?"

"Poison?" James asked shocked.

Cayden looked at his mother. "Is that true?"

"I just wanted to speed up the process, dear. It was Belinda that was behind this ultimate betrayal."

"Mother, you have a lot of explaining to do" Cayden replied.

"Angie I should have listened to you about Belinda", James said color returning to his face. I knew something was off but couldn't quite figure it out."

"It's ok James, I will explain more but you were under a spell, so it wasn't completely all your fault".

He smiled slightly at the dig it warmed my heart to see him smile.

"Cayden, I'm so sorry. I care for you very much, but I can't marry you. That is not what I want, but I genuinely hope that you will still be part of my life."

"Angie," Cayden started to say.

"It's Angel to you," I said, smiling.

Cayden smiled back at me and nodded.

"What nonsense, child. Look at all you can do! We can train you to use your powers correctly," Mrs. Montgomery said.

"I think I've got this now, thanks." I turned to James. "We better get back to the cabin quick, so no one suspects. As for all of them …" I looked up at the ceiling. "You created them, it's now up to you to decide their fate." I waved my hand, and they fell hard onto the ground.

Belinda was first up to start groveling at Mrs. Montgomery's feet.

Bright red and gold tendrils came out of my mark and surrounded James and me, and we flew down a vortex and landed safely in the cabin.

"You've got some more explaining to do cadet, how did you do that?" James said.

"All in good time, I promise," I said, and kissed him deeply. He kissed me back.

"What happened to your lip?" he asked.

I had forgotten about that. I raised my palm to it, and a slight glow healed it good as new.

"Nothing," I said, grinning.

"But…"

"Quick, they'll be here soon. Handcuff me."

"Yes, ma'am."

Not a second after I sat down with my cuffed hands, we heard Reggie's voice.

"This is Cadet Pickard of The New York Police Academy, come out with your hands up. We know you're in there."

I smiled. "Right on cue."

"Let's go home cadet," James said.

He helped me up and through the front door.

"I surrender," James said. He knelt on the ground and spread his hands out so they could see them.

Reggie and Jay rushed forward holding their weapons, saying and doing the exact right things. Reggie read James his rights, and Jay took me over to a paramedic, asking for my statement on events.

If only I could tell her the true events—now, that would be one for the records.

EXPLANATION

James and I sat in the mess hall, me with a steaming hot chocolate and him with coffee. It was late, but neither of us was ready for bed yet. Jay and Reggie had passed the final assessment with flying colors. They impressed the instructors by deciding to work together—a first in the Academy History—and they found us in record time, beating the record by a full hour.

James put his hand on mine, my new angel fire glowing happily. He turned my hand over, rubbing my mark, which was a more distinct shape now.

"I owe you an explanation," I said.

"I know it's hard. I'm happy to wait 'til the time is right for you," James said.

"I'm ready to start." I smiled at him.

"For the longest time since I can remember, I've been able to look into people and see who they are. I was good at finding the darkness, but I realize now people are a lot better than bad. I hadn't fully embraced the good in me to see that and accept the love and help around me." I looked into James' eyes. "There is still more I need to understand, and a lot more to tell you."

"We can figure it out together," he said as he leaned in to kiss me. His lips were so soft on mine. I think we could have stayed like that forever, but eventually; I pulled back.

"Right, cadet," he said and smiled. "You better rest for another big day tomorrow."

I didn't want to leave him, it hurt to be parted so soon but reluctantly we parted and I left the mess.

Jay was already asleep. I'd told her I would catch her up on James's tomorrow; she couldn't help but notice the looks between us.

Glowing by my bed was a green demogram. I opened it immediately.

Angel, you will always be in my heart. —Cx

I smiled, and for the first time, conjured one myself. I did a soft giggle. An Angelgram. Mine was glowing a soft white. I swirled my finger loosely over it to make a symbol of angel wings on fire, and sent it to him, knowing he would be impressed.

Next to Cayden's demogram was a postcard from my dad.

I picked it up and smiled.

Dear Angel, I hope this gets there in time before your big day. I just wanted to say I am so proud of you and know your mother would be too. We will always be there for you no matter what. See you soon!

—Dad.

LAST DAY

No alarm woke me up the next morning; instead, it was Jay. "Angie, wake up."

"Huh?" I sat up. "Has something happened?"

She smiled. "It may have taken me the whole course, but I'm awake for the run."

"There is no run this morning," I said, confused.

"You're right, there isn't one as part of the course, but it's the last time we can all run together before we graduate."

I smiled back at her. "Let's do it."

Outside in the chilly morning air, it seemed like we were not the only ones.

Mike and Reggie came around the corner. I smiled.

"Damn body clock," Reggie said as his breath lingered in the chilly air.

At the track, James stood there waiting for us.

"How did you know?" Jay asked.

"Well cadet, I didn't, but I knew one day you would see how much you have improved and become part of this place, just like we could see it. I wanted to be there for that moment for you."

Jay looked at all of us, grinning at her.

"Okay okay, don't get all mushy. Can we run already?" She smiled too.

James got out his stopwatch.

"For the very last time as New York Police Cadets, on your mark, get set, go!'

I stood in my mirror. The same blue eyes looked back, but I felt different, stronger. I smoothed down an unseen wrinkle from my crisply ironed uniform. I had stood here for the last six months doing this same thing. I was different. The woman looking back at me had always been there, but I hadn't been ready to see her. This was me. I smiled. In my reflection, two golden wings glowed. I glowed, and through that glow was a swirling fire.

"You're beautiful," I whispered to my angel fire.

"I know, right!" Jay exclaimed, bounding into the bathroom.

I looked at Jay, impressed. "Wow, look at the shine on those shoes!"

She beamed. "This is it, Angie."

"Are you nervous?" I asked.

"Hell yes! I haven't seen my parents or brother and sister since we started. I think I was a bit of a brat then."

I laughed. "Maybe just a bit. But they're going to be so proud of you!"

"I would hug you but I don't want to get crinkly. So, what's the plan after this for you and James?"

"We're going to take it slow. I need to introduce him to my dad first."

"Oh yeah. Don't worry, he'll love him!"

"I hope so."

Jay grabbed my hands "Before we go, I just wanted to thank you for all of your support."

"Jay, I…" I started.

"Let me finish. I mean it, Angie. You always just let me be me and I know I can be pretty annoying."

I smiled. "You aren't, you know."

"But seriously, thanks for pushing me in the right places and, you know, being there."

I sniffed. "Ditto. There's so much more I want to tell you."

"I know, but it's okay. I'm not going anywhere. Besides, we're going to be roommates!"

I rolled my eyes. "Maybe I didn't think that one through."

"Can't go back now." Jay beamed. "You'll see. It will be loads of fun."

"I hope we get our first solo assignments to the same division!"

"Me too," I said. "Okay, let's do this."

We looked at our room for the last time, and walked out to our ceremony, hand in hand.

GRADUATION

My hands were sweating buckets into my dress gloves. We stood outside, waiting to go into the auditorium.

Our families had arrived. We weren't allowed to see them until after graduation.

Madison Square Garden was huge, and I couldn't believe our graduation was here. It was tradition. I crouched down, trying to calm my nerves.

"Those gold braids weighing you down, Whitewing?" Reggie smiled at me, holding out his hand. I reached out and took it.

"I could say the same thing to you," I said, smiling back.

"Well, if I had to come second to someone, I'm glad it's you." Reggie smiled. The Academy only gave gold braids to cadets that scored 98% in their classes.

"Sshhhh, you two, it's showtime. Let's get this over with so we can go celebrate already!" Jay said to us.

The grand doors ahead of us opened. My fire started pumping. *It's okay. We knew Mrs. Montgomery would be here.*

The song "New York, New York" started to blare out as we all marched in.

On stage sat all of the dignitaries close to the Academy. Mrs. Montgomery sat in the very front row, Cayden next to her, smiling. Her "scarf" turned its head to wink at me as I marched past.

At the podium, Reggie's father stood, ready to address us. I didn't know where my dad or James was, but I could sense they were both there. We got to our allocated seats and were instructed to sit. Jay was on my left and Reggie was on my right. I felt so proud of them.

The Police Commissioner walked up to the podium. "Welcome cadets, and welcome to everyone who could come today to our graduation ceremony. Before we start, I would like you all to stand for our nation's national anthem. Singing this will be Cadet Price."

Jay stood up next to me. I turned and whispered to her, "I didn't know you could sing. For real?!" Jay blushed slightly and marched to the stage.

As we all stood there saluting, Jay's golden voice sang out strongly as a video played across the giant screens in front of us. It was us! They showed the pain and the work of the family that sat here with me.

Jay's voice died away, and for thirty seconds, no one moved. Then the spell broke, and everyone couldn't help but applaud her as she made her way off stage. I sniffed and wiped the tears from my eyes.

I couldn't speak, just nodded as she sat back next to me. She grabbed my hand in acknowledgment.

"Thank you, Cadet Price. Perhaps after that performance, you should consider being part of our department's designated National Anthem Singers."

Jay blushed.

"Next, I would love to introduce to you our class valedictorian. Before she comes up here, I'm going to embarrass her a bit." Everyone laughed. I looked down at the floor, my hands sweating bullets.

"Some may say this cadet is stubborn; we say she's tenacious. Some might say she takes too many risks, while we say she's brave. Some might say she's an overachiever, but we say she's a leader. And some—myself included—may have underestimated her, only to be proven wrong on several occasions. This talented Cadet has received the Purple Heart of Bravery while in training, which is a first, and achieved the highest overall average score in every discipline, including a first for this academy, in physical fitness. Cadet Whitewing, please make your way to the stage."

The applause was deafening as I made my way up, and I could now see my dad and James standing up, clapping. They were next to each other. I walked past Mrs. M and Cayden on the stage and turned my back on them to address my police family.

"When I first joined the Academy, I felt lost, searching for answers. 'Who am I? Will I make a difference? Will I make those close to me proud?' It wasn't until we were halfway through that I realized I wasn't alone in these questions. We all had the same ones and we answered them together. I am so incredibly proud of each one of you. You are part of my, family, and I would not be standing here today without you. We are making a difference already by graduating today. And who are we? We are New York, Police Officers. Stand up, stand tall. Congratulations!"

THE END

CHRISSY DAWSON

Chrissy is a London based
Kiwi living with her Son and
Husband. As well as being
an Author, Chrissy Dawson
(aka Metge) is also a full
time Film and TV Producer,
having worked on 16 films
and counting, her love of
storytelling grows everyday.

'As a little girl I grew up
with a stack of comic books from my father, this was
Richie Rich, Mickey Mouse and more. I love being part of
bringing stories to life in every medium'.

'Angela WhiteWing came to me as an idea after my son
was born. What if we had the power to see people as they
really are? What would you change?

You can find out more about Chrissy and upcoming books
at http://chrissydawson.com

COMING SOON!

CHRISSY DAWSON

Sign up to our newsletter at:
https://chrissydawson.com/account/register
to get notifications when Book 2,
Angel in Training is available.

Special thanks go out to all the Angels
that have come into my life, you know who you are!

www.ingramcontent.com/pod-product-compliance
Lightning Source LLC
Chambersburg PA
CBHW021159110726
47900CB00002B/650